SATAN'S PONY

SATAN'S

THOMAS DUNNE BOOKS
ST. MARTIN'S MINOTAUR ➤ NEW YORK

PONY

ROBIN HATHAWAY

To
J.J. and Eff-Eff

THOMAS DUNNE BOOKS.
An imprint of St. Martin's Press

www.minotaurbooks.com

Library of Congress Cataloging-in-Publication Data

Hathaway, Robin
  Satan's pony / Robin Hathaway.—1st ed.
    p. cm.
  ISBN 0-312-33322-6
  EAN 978-0312-3322-5
  1. Women physicians—Fiction. 2. Motorcyclists—Crimes against—Fiction.
3. Travelers—Services for—Fiction. 4. New Jersey—Fiction. I. Title.

PS3558.A7475S25 2004
813'.54—dc22

2004046800

First Edition: October 2004

10 9 8 7 6 5 4 3 2 1

ACKNOWLEDGMENTS

I am deeply indebted to the following people for their help and encouragement with this novel:

Ruth Cavin, my editor; Laura Langlie, my agent; Bob Keisman, Julie Miller, Anne Keisman, and Jeff Brangan.

Special thanks to Professor Roderick Vosburgh of La Salle University, Sylvia Isaacson, and Michael Crescitelli for their time and expert advice.

Last, but certainly not least, my deepest thanks to Jason J. Miller for his knowledge of bikers and biking, and—for the title of this book.

AUTHOR'S NOTE

It's not my intention to portray bikers as devils incarnate. I know there are bikers of all varieties—from hardened criminals to the Sunday rider who could be your doctor, lawyer, or next-door neighbor.

The Satan's Apostle Club—a creation of pure fiction—lies somewhere in between. It has members who have raped and murdered and others who, although tough, are also kind and generous. But they have all passed the "righteous" test, which, in biker language, means loyalty to the point of death. They will never snitch, squeal, or rat on a brother biker, because this is the eighth "deadly sin," and they are willing to give up their lives for any member of their club. All but one.

THE SATAN'S APOSTLE CLUB ROSTER

PI (as in 3.14), *President*—mathematician and MIT dropout

STARS AND STRIPES, *Sergeant-at-Arms*—a Marine and most feared disciplinarian

JINGLES, *Treasurer*—sticky fingers, but in charge of club funds as a test

MICKEY—comic book artist

HASH BROWN—short-order cook

SAWHORSE—construction worker

HONEY—sweetest guy, unless you mention his mother

HAMMERHEAD—one-man wrecking crew

FOXHOLE—Nam veteran. Oldest member

ORPHEUS—guitar player

LIGHTNING—fastest rider

SUNNY—sex machine

O! beware, my lord, of jealousy;
It is the green ey'd monster . . .

—IAGO, from *Othello*

MONDAY

CHAPTER 1

Nobody knew where they came from. All anyone wanted to know was—when were they leaving?

They'd arrived like a cloud of hornets late Sunday afternoon and taken over the parking lot and most of the motel rooms. I'd heard them come in—*rowrrrrrgh, rowrrrrrgh, rowrrrrrgh*—one after the other. I'd jumped up from my futon, where I'd been relaxing to the strains of Miles Davis, and looked out my window at the string of bikes gleaming below me in the sun. The bikers' helmets gleamed, too—every color of the rainbow. My first reaction was a rush of excitement; the second—a stab of irritation, as I realized that this was the end of peace and tranquillity at the Oakview Motor Lodge.

Here it was Monday morning, and the "Satan's Apostles" (the name embroidered in red across the backs of their leather vests) showed no signs of moving on. In fact, Jack-the-Night-Clerk told me in an awed whisper, "They've signed up for the whole week!" It had been an unusually warm May, and the flat roads and balmy climate (seventy degrees, not a cloud in the sky) of south Jersey seemed to agree with them.

The first time I ran into one, face-to-face, was this morning. I'd shuffled down to the lobby—glassy-eyed, before my morning coffee—to pick up my copy of the *Bayfield Bugle*. I was reaching for it on the counter where Jack always leaves it for me when this *thing* came up next to my elbow and woke me quicker than six cups of coffee and a cold shower.

It was bulky, hairy, noisy, and multicolored. The bulk was muscle, bulging out of a torn T-shirt and battered jeans; the hair, body hair, springing from the arms, chest, and legs as well as long greasy locks sprouting from the head; the noise, bracelets, necklaces, and anklets of heavy metal (yeah—like the music, only more so); and the multicolors, tattoos over every visible surface—red, blue, black, purple, and green.

He was asking where he could get "a decent cuppa coffee," implying that the motel offering wasn't up to his standards (or anybody else's, for that matter). Without thinking (I wasn't awake yet, remember), and before Paul Nelson, the desk clerk and owner, could get the words out, I blurted: "The Blue Arrow."

He turned, and I was treated to the full frontal view. Hair, tattoos, metal. "Where's that?"

I mumbled directions to the local diner.

"Thanks." And he clanked off into the sunset (or in this case—sunrise).

Paul looked at me. I shrugged. I'd been a motel tenant for only eight months, but long enough to take most things with a grain of salt. The thing about motel living was, everything was temporary. Nothing lasted very long. You'd just begin to get in a snit about something, and "poof," it was gone, down the road to the next motel. That was one of the things I liked about motel life. I grabbed my paper, a cup of the motel sludge, and retreated to my apartment. By redecorating and moving in a few pieces of my own furniture, I'd raised the space where I lived from two-star motel to "half-decent apartment."

CHAPTER 2

Slowly I began to change my clothes. From the jeans, tee, and flip-flops I'd thrown on to get the paper to something a little more presentable. I had to go to court this morning and I wasn't looking forward to it.

I'd promised Maggie I'd go with her to the courthouse where she was scheduled to testify about her son's "sterling qualities." Nick was accused of a whole lot of things—smuggling, conspiracy, attempted murder, even successful murder. You name it. He was on trial with a number of other Bayfielders who were involved in an immigrant smuggling ring and sweatshop that I had helped to uncover. A problem kid and chronic drug abuser, Nick had disappeared three years ago. He'd been presumed dead by his parents, Paul and Maggie Nelson, the owners of the Oakview Motor Lodge where I live, until he turned up as the Simon Legree of an immigrant sweatshop.

The Nelsons had been kind to me when I had arrived at Bayfield eight months ago, offering me lodging and office space, not to mention their friendship. In short, I owed them. With a grimace I gave the unaccustomed panty hose a yank up my leg.

The house phone rang.

Letting the panty hose hang, I answered it.

"Jo? The car's here. Please hurry." Maggie's voice, usually strong and steady, was weak and hesitant.

I finished dressing as if on a CODE BLUE and appeared in the lobby three minutes later.

"Come *on*." Maggie's face was pale, and when she grabbed my hand hers was damp and cold. I swallowed the sassy comment I had ready for the normal Maggie and tagged obediently after her to the car.

The Bridgeton courthouse is the largest building in town. In fact, it's the only large building in town. Built in the Federal style in the 1890s, it has a cupola with a copper crown that has weathered over time from golden molasses to pistachio ice cream green. At the moment the building was under construction, and according to Maggie, it had been for about five years. Things moved slowly in the county seat—in the poorest county in New Jersey. In the good old days, Maggie told me, you could stroll in and out of the courthouse without anyone hardly noticing. Now, you had to practically strip before you got one foot in the door.

After being scrutinized, patted, and searched, I asked, "Where do we go?"

Maggie took the lead. She had been coming here daily for the past three weeks and knew her way around.

The interior of the courthouse was a surprise. I had expected dark wooden floors and walls, heavy, forbidding doors, and dim lighting. Instead, the floors were shiny white marble, the walls blond wood with coral trim, and ample light flowed from skylights and a myriad of modern fixtures. The grim aspect of the majority of older courthouses had been completely erased. It would be almost a pleasure to be hauled in here for a crime.

We took a flight of marble steps to the second floor, turned down a bright corridor to the left, and stopped before a polished wooden door labeled in gold: COURTROOM 3. A woman in a fresh blue uniform stood outside, checking IDs. As I presented my card, I heard the murmur of voices on the other side of the door. I began to feel nervous myself. I had forgotten I might have to confront the couple who had captured and tortured me. The Malevolent Milacs. I had successfully blocked on them. I shivered at the memory of them. Later that month, I would have the pleasure of testifying against them—but not today.

As we entered the courtroom, several heads turned. Maggie left me in the spectator section while she pushed through a little swinging gate to join her attorney onstage, as it were. Before she left, she squeezed my hand and whispered, "Thank you."

She looked so vulnerable and un–Maggie-like I whispered back, "You'll do fine."

She bit her lip.

I switched my gaze to the jury: twelve "honest" citizens, decked out in their Sunday best. Sunday was still a big deal in south Jersey and they all had some "best" stored in their closets. The five men were over fifty, with paunches and white or thinning hair. The seven women were late middle-aged, sleepy, and overweight.

There was a stir in the courtroom as a door opened to the left of the judge's bench and a young man was ushered in. Short and stocky with long black hair, he wore an orange jumper over his gray prison garb. Shackles dragged at his ankles and he was helped to a seat by the guard who accompanied him. In the quick glimpse I had of his face, he did not resemble the photograph in Maggie's living room. That youth had worn a surly, arrogant expression. This one smiled serenely, as if just anointed by the Heavenly Host. Maggie had told me that while he was in prison awaiting trial Nick had found the Lord, repented his sins, and claimed to be "born again." Skeptic that I am, I had taken this with a huge grain of salt. But Maggie, although his adoptive mother, fell for the tale hook, line, and sinker.

A minute later a door opened to the right of the bench and the judge came in. He was small and wiry, with the complexion of strong tea. The name on the plaque resting on the lectern read: Torres. The lawyer for the prosecution introduced his first witness. After listening for a few minutes, I figured out that he was a leather expert testifying to the nature of the machinery used in the sweatshop where the immigrants had been forced to work. Ho, hum. I pulled a paperback from my backpack. Maggie had tried to convince me to bring a traditional handbag. I didn't own one. She would lend me one. All of hers were huge and black, like my grandmother used to carry. We compromised. I told her I'd bring my *baby* backpack. Not the big one. She relented.

"Will Margaret Townsend Nelson please take the stand." The clerk of the court's voice rang out clearly.

I sat up with a jolt and my paperback slid to the floor. I dived for it, then raised my gaze to the witness-box.

"Please stand, place your hand on the Bible, and swear: I, Margaret Townsend Nelson, do solemnly swear to tell the truth, the whole truth, and nothing but the truth, so help me God."

It was very unusual to call a mother to testify on her son's behalf. A mother's testimony is rarely reliable and always biased. Everyone knew that. The lawyer was desperate, I guess. Maggie was his last-ditch attempt to evoke some sympathy for the defendant from the jury. I had to lean forward and strain my ears to hear Maggie, whose strident tones usually rang from one end of the motel to the other.

"You may be seated."

Maggie slumped rather than sat. Until now, I hadn't realized how small she was. Although the witness-box was no more than a chair enclosed by four flimsy partitions of blond wood, it seemed to swallow her.

Glancing at her son, Maggie seemed to gain strength. She sat up, lifted her chin, and looked more like the solid, capable innkeeper I was familiar with. I wished I could see Nick's face. Paul Nelson, Nick's father, was conspicuously absent. He, too, had not swallowed the conversion story. When Nick had been arrested, Paul and Maggie had gone to the local jail to see him, and Nick had spit on them. Since then, Paul had not returned and I had never heard him speak his son's name again. Maggie, on the other hand, visited him daily.

The lawyer for the defense stepped up to the witness-box. He was small, dapper, and businesslike. Maggie had told me he was costing them a fortune. "Mrs. Nelson, will you give the jury a brief account of your son?" His tone was brusque.

The jury, which had resembled a bunch of drugged zombies during the leather expert's recital, eyed the new witness with interest.

"Paul and I were never able to have any children," Maggie began in her newly acquired soft voice, staring at her lawyer.

"Please speak up, Mrs. Nelson," the judge ordered, but his tone was kindly, "and address your remarks to the jury."

Maggie obediently turned her head toward the twelve people on her left and raised her voice. "Paul and I were never able to have any children of our own, and when I was forty we decided to adopt." Her gaze slid briefly to her son. "I'll never forget the day we brought him home. He was—"

"Mrs. Nelson, please confine your remarks to your son's later years," her lawyer said, "the years in which his character will have some bearing on the issues at hand."

Whose side is he on?

"Oh . . . sorry." Flustered, she asked, "At what age do you want me to start?"

"Puberty."

She looked bewildered.

"Thirteen," said the judge.

Maggie seemed to go into a trance, to leave the courtroom for some other, happier place.

Come on, Mag! I silently rooted for her. I might not care for her son, but I couldn't bear to see my friend humiliated.

"He was a normal boy. He went to school. He played sports. Soccer was his favorite. Rough-and-tumble. He always liked to roughhouse. Oh, not in any bad way," she added hastily, "just like all boys do." Her voice was gaining strength. "It was hard on him because we were older than most of his friends' parents. We couldn't carry on with him like the younger mothers and fathers did. Sometimes I think he resented this—and was embarrassed to have such old, fuddy-duddy parents." She glanced at her son for affirmation. Again, I wished I could see his face. "Anyway . . . his favorite hobby was tinkering with cars and motors. When he was sixteen he persuaded his father to buy him a motorbike. They didn't tell me anything about it until they brought it home. They knew I wouldn't approve. But when I saw how happy he was with it, I didn't object. He took such good care of it. And he always wore his helmet."

Until he was out of sight, I thought uncharitably. The sudden realization that this same bike now belonged to me caught me up short. The Nelsons had sold it to me for a song, when they had thought their son was dead and would no longer have any use for it. (They were right about the no use part.) It was my sole means of transportation and the way I made my motel calls. I wished she would get on with it. So did the judge, apparently.

"Go on, Mrs. Nelson," he urged her.

Maggie took a deep breath. "He was an average student and graduated in the middle of his class. Graduation Day was a proud day. The boys all looked so handsome. Most of them I'd never seen wear a tie before. . . ."

Her lawyer glanced at his watch.

Does he have an important luncheon date?

"What did your son do after high school?" he asked.

"Well, his dad and I wanted him to go to college. We could have scraped together the money. But he wasn't interested. He said he liked to work with his hands. So he signed up at the local vocational school. He took a course in sanitation engineering."

Plumbing, I translated.

"And did he work as a plumber?" the lawyer translated for the jury.

"For about a year, off and on, until . . ." Her voice faded and she slumped in her chair again.

"Please speak up, Mrs. Nelson. Until what?"

With a great effort, she said, "Until he disappeared."

The members of the jury blinked in unison, as if someone had pushed buttons on the backs of their necks.

"Disappeared?" the lawyer repeated, as if he didn't know the story.

"Paul and I, and our neighbors, searched everywhere. His bike was parked at the motel, so we didn't think he could have gone far. Finally we called the police and they reported him to Missing Persons. The FBI was even called in. . . ."

"Did you think he had been taken against his will?"

"Kidnapped, you mean?"

The lawyer nodded.

"Yes. We both thought so. By those awful people, and they probably hypnotized him, and—"

"How long was he missing?"

Maggie glanced again at her son, and when she spoke it was as if she were dragging the words up from some deep hole. "Three . . . years."

The women on the jury looked sympathetic. One even wiped away a tear.

"So, you see . . ." She sat up and her voice rose. *Now that I've got him back, I can't lose him again!*

I stared at my feet.

"You see, he's sorry now for what he did, running off and leaving us to worry and grieve. And for getting mixed up with those terrible people. It was the drugs that did it. My son would never have acted like that if he was himself. . . ."

The lawyer frowned.

She pressed a hand against her mouth.

Oh, Mag, you just blew the whole kidnapping theory! I groaned.

"But now he's repented," she said, trying to save the day. "He's truly sorry for what he did and wants to make a fresh start." She stared beseechingly at the jury.

One by one, the twelve members looked away.

"Any more questions, Mr. Maxwell?" the judge addressed the lawyer.

"No more questions, Your Honor." The lawyer, deflated, turned away.

"Thank you, Mrs. Nelson," the judge said in a gentler tone. "We'll recess for lunch and reconvene at two o'clock." He gathered his robes about him, preparing to leave.

A woman officer in uniform came to help Maggie from the witness-box. She stumbled on the way out. As the guard led her to her seat, she seemed dazed. I raised my hand to wave but let it fall back in my lap. She wouldn't have seen it anyway.

CHAPTER 3

I had told Maggie I couldn't stay for the afternoon session. I had office hours. I was sorry because I knew she would have to face the prosecutor and a grilling much worse than this morning's. I got a lift back to the motel with one of the spectators who happened also to be one of my patients.

The motel parking lot swarmed with half-naked tattooed bruisers with beer cans that seemed to be soldered to their hands. The way they joshed and roughhoused together reminded me of a bunch of junior high school kids, only bigger, as if they'd sampled some of that magic potion in Alice's Wonderland.

As I edged my way through the lobby, carefully dodging them, Paul Nelson called me over. "Hey, Jo!"

He looked tired. Already worn out worrying about Maggie, he now had to deal with this hoard of noisy, brainless, unwashed bums that had descended on him.

"Could you do me a favor?" he asked.

"You name it," I said.

"Keep an eye on Mag. I have to go up to the city for some supplies." ("The city" always meant Philadelphia, not Bridgeton.) "I don't like leaving her here with . . ." he said, and nodded at the crowd.

"I'll watch her like a hawk," I assured him. He didn't ask how her testimony had gone, I noted. He had shut himself off from that aspect of her life, as if it didn't exist. I wondered how Paul kept this up at home. Could he actually sit through a whole meal with Maggie without asking about her day—or his son? But my knowledge of married life was skimpy, as I'd been raised by a single parent—my father. My mother died when I was four. I was totally ignorant of the games, the little subterfuges, the lies, and the silences employed by husbands and wives.

"Thanks," Paul said. "How do you like our new guests?" He winked.

"Nothing like a full house!" I gave him a thumbs-up.

Ignoring the whistles and catcalls, I threaded my way through the throng. If I kept my gaze straight ahead and my mouth shut, maybe I could make it to the door without incident. There were only twelve of them, Jack had told me. But because of their size and the racket they made in the small lobby, it seemed more like twenty. It wasn't until I reached the parking lot that I broke my vow. I was revving my bike when this bruiser on a gorgeous midnight blue Harley rolled up beside me. From under droopy lids he eyed my sad little secondhand Honda, grinning.

"What's so funny?" I snapped.

"Nothin'." He cast another pitying glance at my bike.

"Up yours!" I took off in a spray of gravel, hoping some of it hit him in the eye.

I was headed for the Blue Arrow and a bite to eat before office hours. But when I arrived, there were three Harleys parked out front. I decided to skip lunch and turned my bike toward home. My office was located in a wooden cabin to one side of the modern concrete hulk of a motel. There were three cabins, throwbacks to the days when the Oakview Motor Lodge was "Oakview Cabins" and the automobile was a novelty. When I'd first arrived, Paul had offered cabin number "1" to me for an office, as part of his lure to get me to stay. The cabin had been in terrible shape. But, with a little carpentry and a lot of paint, I had rehabbed it into an acceptable office and waiting room. I even had a steady trickle of patients that helped my main source of income—the motel trade. I provided health care to the guests of a number of motels in the area and made my calls on my motorbike. The locals called me Motel Doctor, but I preferred to think of myself as a general practitioner. When I had practiced in New York with a swanky group at an elite big-name hospital, I had been a pediatrician. But the death of a child, due to my misdiagnosis, had humbled me and sent me packing to the wilds of south Jersey. I still hadn't come to grips with my guilt over Sophie. But I was working on it. Maybe one day . . .

Bayfield lay in a remote part of rural Jersey, on the Delaware Bay. Isolated and thinly populated, it had a distinctive beauty all its own. In the spring, the fields turned a shade of green that rivaled the Emerald City of Oz. And in the fall, instead of the flashy reds and oranges of New England, the trees turned softer shades of rose, lavender, and gold.

It was the sky that hooked me. Growing up around Manhattan, I hadn't seen much of it. Here, instead of snatching little peeks of blue between buildings, you had sky to spare. It spread around you like a huge shawl, changing color according to the weather. In Manhattan, the Chrysler Building had been my weathercock. On gray days it was a dull pewter and when the sun shone it sparkled like a jeweled crown. I still missed it. Bayfield, however, has a serene quality with a healing power that I needed right now. At least it *did* have—until the Satan's Apostles arrived!

When I came in the office there were three patients waiting. The first was Esther Lockweed, the local gossip. As healthy as a horse, and weighing about the same, she had probably dreamed up some bogus ailment in order grill me about the trial. I determined to keep her visit short.

When she was seated, I asked, "What seems to be the trouble?"

"Oh, the usual aches and pains. My left knee is swelled up something terrible." She yanked up her skirt, revealing a plump knee that was slightly swollen.

"I've told you—"

"I know; I know. I should lose weight. But you don't know how hard it is when you love to cook and eat as much as I do," she whined.

"Are you taking your *Voltarin*?"

She nodded. "But it doesn't do much good. Can't you give me something stronger?"

I opened a drawer at my side, drew out her file, and studied it.

"You've been over to the courthouse?" she asked.

I gave a brusque nod.

"How's Maggie doing?"

"She's doing fine. I think we can increase your—"

"Has she taken the stand yet?"

"Yes. We can increase your dose to—"

"When will *he* be taking the stand?"

I put her file down. "You know, Mrs. Lockweed, the trial is open to the public. You could go and see for your—"

"Oh, I couldn't do that. Go and gawk at my neighbors when they're in trouble?"

"Maggie's not in trouble." I bristled.

"No, but her son—"

I slapped Mrs. Lockweed's file folder shut and scribbled a prescription. "Fill this at your local pharmacy." I handed it to her and stood up. "And have a nice day."

Sarcasm was lost on Mrs. Lockweed.

"Do you think he really did those awful things?"

I turned away, intent on replacing her file in the drawer.

With a sigh, she lumbered out.

The next two patients were men—farmers who only spoke when spoken to. What a relief. I was through with them in a jiffy. As I was cleaning up, I heard the outer door open. *Damn*. I thought I was finished for the day.

"Gotta a cure for lovesickness?" Tom Canby poked his handsome head around the door.

I laughed. "Hi, stranger." I hadn't heard from him for three days. Very unusual.

"It's archery season. I got me a deer."

I had once been put off by his hunting habit, but that was before I knew how destructive deer could be.

He grabbed me by both shoulders and gave me a long, deep kiss.

"Hey!" I broke free. "I'm still working."

He glanced around the empty office.

I looked at my watch. "Office hours are from two to four. It's only three forty-five. Somebody might drop in."

He slid into the chair opposite me—the one reserved for patients or drug salesmen (although very few of the latter found their way to Bayfield). "Well, Doc, it's this way," he began, giving a good imitation of a local redneck. "I cain't sleep, I cain't eat, and my heart goes pitter-patter so fast—"

"That's called palpitations."

"Whatever." He frowned. "Why aren't you takin' notes, Doctor?"

"Idiot."

Undeterred, he went on, "But the worst thing is my feet."

"Huh?"

"Every time I think of you my feet itch." He pulled off his shoes and socks and wriggled his bare toes at me. (They were nice toes.) "Like right now, for instance."

"Maybe you have athlete's foot."

He shook his head. "I'm no ath-a-lete. The only sport I know is archery, and my feet don't get involved much in that."

"Maybe I have some foot powder here. . . ." I made a pretense of rummaging in my medicine cabinet.

"Tried that. Don't work," he said. "The only cure is a house call to my place—at, say, eight o'clock?"

"How's that going to help your feet?"

He grinned. "That's for me to know and you to find out."

"Well . . . if you've discovered some new antidote?"

"Oh, I can't say it's *new*. But it's tried and true. Very effective."

"FDA-approved?"

"Oh, yeah. For years."

"Hmm. Let me think about it."

"Shall I give you a sample?"

"Uh . . ."

He bounded around the desk and grabbed me.

By the time he left, it was four-thirty. As I locked my office door, it occurred to me that bikers weren't the only people in Bayfield who acted like junior high kids.

CHAPTER 4

Before going to my room to change, I checked the lobby to see if Maggie had dropped by. Jack was on desk duty and said he hadn't seen her. When I got to my room I called her at home. She answered, sounding exhausted.

"How did it go?" I asked.

"Not good, I'm afraid."

"What happened?"

"The prosecutor only questioned me for about five minutes . . ."

That could be a good or bad sign. Good if it kept Maggie from putting her foot in it again. Bad if the prosecutor thought she had done enough damage to the defendant and no further testimony was needed.

". . . and my lawyer hardly spoke to me afterward. I think he was disgusted with me."

From what I'd seen of Mr. Maxwell, Esq., that was probably indifference, not disgust. "He may have had other things on his mind. Have you eaten?"

"I grabbed a burger on the way home."

"Well, go to bed early."

"Yes, Doctor."

A glimmer of humor? A good sign. "When will Paul be home?" I asked.

"I just heard him drive up."

"Take care, Mag."

I arrived at Tom's place a little after eight. He was sitting on the screen porch nursing a beer when I pulled up. Registering no surprise, he continued to sit while I dismounted. He had been expecting me. As I came up the steps, he rose and headed for the fridge.

"Make mine a soda. I'm on call tonight," I said.

Tom's porch ran east to west along one side of the house. You could catch the sunrise or sunset by just turning in your chair. He'd planned it that way when he built the house. It was a simple frame house, with two large rooms, a kitchen, and a bath. When I'd first met him, he had told me modestly that he was a carpenter. But he was really an architect. He made his living rehabbing old houses in south Jersey—breathing new life into them.

He brought me a frosty Coke. I took the other chair. There were only two—both wicker rockers badly in need of paint. We sipped and rocked and watched the sun go down. By this time of day it had run out of steam and was taking its quiet leave with pale streaks of pink and gold. The fields darkened quickly. It was hard to tell where the fields ended and the sky began—until the stars popped out.

I told Tom about the trial, Nick, and Maggie.

"Poor Mag," he said. He had gone through high school with Nick, was a close friend of the family, and knew the whole sad story.

Then I told him about the bikers.

"Ohmygod!" he slapped his forehead. "You'd better move in with me." He had been prodding me to do this for some time now. I wasn't ready.

"It's not *that* bad," I said.

"Thanks." He feigned insult.

Again we fell silent and I felt his gaze on me in the dark—as if it had form, texture, and warmth.

"What about this foot cure of yours?" I spoke lightly.

"I thought you'd never ask." Setting down his beer, he knelt at my feet. He removed my boots and both socks. "Up we go!" He pulled me up and led me to a corner of the porch. This was where he kept his bed in summer, a mattress and a pillow, covered with a patchwork quilt. The quilt was the genuine article, made by his great-great-grandmother, he'd told me. Folding it carefully, he hung it on the back of one of the chairs. He fluffed the pillow once and said, "Lie down."

I lay down.

Gently he began to message my right foot.

"But you're the one with the itchy feet," I protested feebly.

"It may seem strange, but it helps *my* feet to massage yours," he said. "It's a new treatment, called 'pedlepathy.'"

"Never heard of it." I closed my eyes.

He switched to the left foot. "Did you know," he said in a low, confidential tone, "that the nerve endings of the feet can affect every part of the body?"

"Reflexology. . . ." I was drifting off.

"But eventually," he continued, "you have to leave the feet— and move on."

"Umm . . . what's that called?"

"Never mind." Slowly his hands moved up my ankles, over my calves, grazed my thighs, and paused at my waist. He was searching for the snap on my jeans when my cell phone rang.

"Damn." I sat up.

"Don't answer it," he said.

"I have to. I'm on call." I dug out my cell and listened to the message. "An accident—at Possum Hollow and Gum Tree roads," I repeated the message. As I scrambled for my socks and boots, I said, "I'm sorry." And I was.

From the porch he watched me mount my bike. When I started the motor he shouted over the roar, "Next time I'm falling for a librarian!"

. . .

Every now and then I wished I *were* a librarian. Someone with regular hours who could count on time for herself. But I also liked the rush of the emergency call. The sudden jerking alive. The surge of adrenaline. The risk and the challenge. Something I had in common with those bozos back at the motel.

Another thing we had in common—I loved to ride. And I especially loved to ride at night. Next to flying in an open cockpit, this must be the closest you can get to becoming one with the universe—fusing with the wind and stars. As the soft air caressed me and the stars sparkled above me, I wished for the second time that I wasn't on call. I wished I could ride all night.

Up ahead, the red lights of an emergency vehicle whirled. Parked nearby was a state police car and another car. I pulled over and reached for my medical kit.

"Dr. Banks here," I told the first medic. He was bending over a small mound by the side of the road.

He looked up with an expression of deep relief. "He's bad, Doc. We were afraid to move him."

I knelt by the small figure lying on his side, eyes closed. A bicycle lay on its side a few yards away. The red lights revolved, washing the boy's face with crimson, over and over. He looked about twelve. I bent, listening for a heartbeat and feeling for a pulse at the same time. There was a faint beat, and a fainter pulse. The kid was unconscious. Severe concussion, I diagnosed. I said, "We've got to get him to the hospital. Move him, but take it easy. I'll follow behind."

The two medics went carefully to work. The whole time I was examining the boy, I had heard a male voice raving on the other side of the road, "I didn't see him. He didn't have any lights. I didn't see him. . . ."

My heart went out to the poor bastard. One of my greatest fears was that I might hit a child while driving at night. How could you ever forgive yourself? Even if it wasn't your fault.

. . .

A CT scan revealed a subdural hematoma—a collection of blood between the layers of the thick protective coverings of the brain. A neurosurgeon was brought from Wilmington by helicopter, removed the fluid between the dura and the skull, and went back to Wilmington. The boy remained unconscious. There was nothing to do now but wait. The parents had been brought in by a neighbor; they were too boozy to drive. They'd been drinking and playing poker on the back porch. Had no idea their boy had gone for a ride . . .

Why not?

. . . but they were ready to sue the driver who sat hunched at the other end of the waiting room, his head in his hands. Around 2:00 AM I took him a cup of coffee. "You should go home. You can't do any good here."

"I wasn't going fast. Honest to God. It was dark. *I didn't see him!*"

The parents were staring at us. "You should go," I said again. "I'll call you if there's any change."

He stumbled to his feet, sloshing coffee on the floor.

"Where can I reach you?"

He fumbled for a pen and paper and scribbled his phone number.

"Try to get some sleep." *Sure. And turn into a pumpkin while you're at it.*

I hung around all night, checking with the nurse for vital signs. Not very professional. But losing a child is hard on any doctor, and especially hard on me. Although this case was not similar in any way to the one that had led me to Bayfield, and certainly not my fault, the feelings about Sophie came rushing back.

The boy—his name was Bobby Shoemaker—was still unconscious at 6:00 AM. I told his parents to go home. The hospital would call them if there was any change. When the morning shift arrived, I knew it was time for me to go, too. Way overtime.

TUESDAY

CHAPTER 5

When I got back to the motel I was not in a good mood. The sight of a bunch of tattooed, half-naked, muscle-bound bruisers milling around the lobby did nothing to improve it. For twelve hours I had forgotten they existed. Now, one stood between me and a much-needed cup of coffee.

"Move!" I grunted.

The assembled company turned and stared.

"Anything left in that pot or have you lapped up the last drop?"

In the beginning they had all looked alike, but little by little distinctive characteristics began to emerge, like with the Seven Dwarfs. You remember that crew—Sleepy, Happy, Grumpy, Dopey, Sneezy, Bashful, and Doc? Only the bikers' nicknames should have been more like Sexy, Boozy, Randy, Sleazy—oh, Dopey would do—and Doc. I think "Doc" would suit their leader just fine. He was the only one who seemed to have any brains, and his eyes, when they were fully open—like now—were more than intelligent. They were an electric, magnetic . . . blue, exuding power. It was a second before I realized he was the same guy that had insulted my bike in the parking lot. But at that time he had been wearing shades, hiding his finest feature.

He made a big deal of getting me a Styrofoam cup, filling it, and asking, "Milk or sugar, ma'am?"

"Straight," I muttered.

He handed it to me with a mock bow. His cronies, who had been watching this performance, guffawed.

Before he could offer the paper plate with two doughnuts, I moved to the other side of the room and collapsed on the end of the sofa. I had intended to go right to my room and crash, but I had a stubborn streak: I didn't want these guys to think they could drive me away.

A middle-aged couple occupied the rest of the sofa—the only nonbikers in residence. They had checked in before the horde arrived and I was surprised they were still here. She was pretty, in a plastic sort of way. Permed hairdo, too-bright makeup, good body, but too much of it on display. She wore a haltertop and short shorts, and when a biker glanced her way (which they often did) she demurely lowered her gaze. Her husband, a stubby, jowly, morose man, sat beside her, watching every move she made.

"Are you the doctor?"

Half-asleep, at first I didn't realize she was speaking to me.

"My husband has an upset stomach and I wondered—"

"Fran, please, I'm fine," the husband protested.

"Well, you weren't *fine* last night, Stan." Her voice rose an octave.

"These things pass," he muttered.

"Sorry." She rolled her eyes, letting me in on the big secret— husbands can be a pain.

They *both* gave me a royal pain. I gulped my coffee and glanced around for the trash can that was always next to the sofa. A biker had confiscated it, turned it upside down, and planted his fat butt on it. I looked for somewhere else to put my cup.

"Let me." A biker with a mop of dirty yellow hair reached for it, in an awkward imitation of Doc's earlier, smoother performance.

I held on.

His hand stayed around the cup *and* my hand—a little too long. I pulled away, starting a tug-of-war.

"Whatcha doin', Sunny?" Doc came up.

Sunny let go.

"Just helpin' the lady out." He moved quickly away, landing in the space I had just vacated on the sofa.

The plastic chick cast him a coy smile. Her husband looked on nervously. I had to get out of here. Succumbing to a mammoth yawn, I staggered toward the door.

Doc was in my way again. "Long night?"

I nodded.

"Want to talk?"

"No, thanks." To my surprise, I was almost tempted to tell him about Bobby.

"I owe you an apology," he said.

I looked at him.

His gaze strayed over my shoulder. "Just a minute. . . ." He pushed past me toward the sofa and grabbed Sunny by the shirt, pulling him up.

These guys are so damned physical.

"What's up?" Sunny looked outraged.

The chick was pop-eyed.

Doc gave Sunny a shove in the direction of the door and followed him out. Everyone was looking at them. An ultimate humiliation for Sunny. After the door closed behind them, there was a moment of silence. Through the half-open window, I could hear Doc chewing Sunny out, but his tone was more like a Dutch Uncle than a biker bully. Then the raucous shouts and laughter resumed, drowning him out.

When Doc returned, he came back to me. "That's a nice bike you have." He continued to talk as if nothing had happened. "I shouldn't have made fun of it. But you should keep it in better shape."

My eyebrows shot up and my mouth fell open.

"Come on. I'll show you what I mean."

Mesmerized by his magnetic gaze and commanding tone, I followed him into the parking lot.

"If you're going to own decent equipment, you've got to take care of it," he scolded. "And don't tell me you don't have time. It needs a lube job. Your exhaust stinks. And it wouldn't hurt to wash it now and then. I bet you've forgotten what color it is."

"I never knew," I admitted.

"It's green. A cool shade of forest green."

"How do you know?"

"I inspected it this morning. I scraped an inch of shit off with my thumbnail. Presto! Forest green." We had reached my bike. "See?"

I stared at the little patch of green.

"Look here!" He squatted on the asphalt, pulling me down beside him.

"Hey," I protested, "I have—"

"Nothing better to do," he finished for me, and began pointing out more defects. He had produced a tool kit and began unscrewing various parts of my bike. Before I knew what was happening, it was lying on the asphalt, totally useless.

"Hey! What if I have an emergency?"

"You can use mine."

I almost wished for an emergency. A ride on that midnight blue hog would be a thrill.

"Does this rice burner have a name?"

"Rice burner?"

"Jap bike."

"Linus," I said.

He frowned, puzzled.

"As in *Peanuts*."

"Oh, yeah. He's the smart one."

"The practical one."

"What's practical about a bike?" He turned to look at me.

I met his gaze. "It's a mode of transportation. It gets me where I want to go. What's the name of yours?"

He sent me a wicked grin. "Satan's Pony."

"Ah. . . ."

"*My* bike is power, risk, danger, escape." He sat up, pointing his wrench at me. "It's freedom!" He went back to work. "By the way," he muttered, "what's practical about waiting around for 'The Great Pumpkin'?"

He was up on his *Peanuts*. I hadn't expected that.

While he worked he talked. He told me they had just had a big funeral for one of their buddies. "Crazy Freddy. It rained the whole time."

"Did you have a tent?"

He made a face. "Tents are for wusses. If it rains, you get wet. Rain is one of the four elements."

"Is that part of your Code?"

He stopped working. "What?"

"The Code. You have one, don't you?"

"What do you know about our Code?"

"Nothing. I just know bikers always have one—like pirates."

He grabbed my wrist. "What d'you know about it?"

"Hey, let go. I'm not one of your old ladies." I tried to pry his fingers off my arm.

"Answer me."

"I read about the Hells Angels' Code in a magazine . . ."

"You're kiddin'." He relaxed his grip.

". . . and I thought the Satan's Apostles must have one, too."

"I always knew the Angels were wusses." He grinned.

I rubbed the flesh above my wrist.

His laugh erupted from somewhere below his diaphragm and rolled across the parking lot. Stopping abruptly, he looked at me. "You'd never read about the Apostles' Code in a magazine," he said.

I changed the subject. "Tell me about Freddy's funeral."

"It was in York, PA. About a hundred of us rode in. I went there from Wyoming."

"Wyoming?" He made it sound like Camden.

"Freddy was crazy as hell. We all take chances, but Freddy out-did us all. He'd slide under riggers and make U-turns on I-95. Nobody could touch Freddy for stunts."

"I guess he tried one stunt too many, huh?"

"Nah. Some drunk clipped him on a back road and he rammed into a tree." He looked somber.

"I'm . . . sorry."

"Yeah. Well, when the word got out we rode in from seventeen states and gave him a hell of a send-off. It took us two days to dig the hole. It had to be big enough for both of them." He was working on my bike again.

"Both of them?"

"Sure. You wouldn't want to part Freddy from his bike. That would be heresy. He'd come back and haunt you." He was applying grease now. "We sat him on the seat, leaning way over the bars, the way he always rode. No helmet. He never wore one. We had two bands playin'. One rock and one heavy metal. They took turns playin' his favorites while we covered him up and drank. A couple of the boys fell in but we pulled 'em out. After the ceremony we gave him a thunderhead."

"Thunderhead?"

"Over a hundred of us roared through the town at top speed. It's our finest tribute. You should of heard it."

The sun was bearing down on us. It felt more like July than May. We were both sweating, but he didn't seem to notice.

"Who are all these guys?" I asked. "Where do your gang members come from?"

"*Club* members," he said sternly.

"Sorry. Club members."

"They come from all over. See this rocker." He pointed to a patch on his vest, under the one with the club logo. It read: NOMADS. "That means we have no home base. We're always on the road." He tackled another bolt. "Sunny, the one with the mop of yellow hair, was an actor in the Big Apple. But he couldn't keep his pecker in his pants. He's a good kid, but those starlets were too much for him. One was underage and he ended up having to leave town. You saw the way he was hitting up that married chick in the lobby this morning. I had to throw him out. He promised me he'd stick to single chicks over eighteen. It's less messy."

"So much for Sunny. What about the others?" I prodded.

"Jingles, the guy with the red beard, he was a card counter. Used to work a blackjack table in Vegas. But he had itchy fingers. Couldn't keep his hand out of the till. Mickey, he's a comic book artist from Dallas. Boy, can he draw. Still sends stuff out freelance. Hash Brown was a short-order cook in Louisville. Sawhorse was in construction in Chicago. These guys still pick up work here and there when we're not on the road. In the winter. Honey's the sweetest. He'd do anything for you as long as you don't mention his mother—"

"What's wrong with his mother?"

"Nothin'. She was raped by a robber when he was a kid. He still feels guilty because he didn't stop the guy. He was only six years old for Christ's sake."

I tried to call up faces to match these anecdotes, but the only one I'd met, if you could call it that, was Sunny.

"Stars and Stripes is a Marine. Here, hold this."

I held the wrench while he stretched out on his belly reaching for an especially awkward nut. When he sat up he said, "Who did I forget?"

I shook my head. "I lost count."

"Hammerhead. He's a real dunce, but he can lift or bust anything. A good man to have around when you're wrecking a bar. Then there's Foxhole—our old man. He was in 'Nam. And Orpheus . . ."

"Orpheus? That's a fancy tag for a biker," I said rudely.

He ignored me. "Orph plays the guitar. Then there's Lightning. No one can beat him for speed. Used to be into race cars but switched to bikes. Said he didn't like all that cage around him. I think that's the lot." He wiped the sweat from his forehead with a beefy arm.

"What about you? What's your tag?" I asked.

"Pi."

"As in apple or three point one four?"

He gave me an enigmatic smile.

"I'll give you a better one," I said. "Doc."

His eyebrows shot up. "I don't get it."

"From the Seven Dwarfs. He was their leader. By the way, how did you get to be the leader?"

He shrugged.

"You're not the biggest."

"Nope."

"Or the prettiest."

"Aw gee. . . ."

"The smartest?"

He was intent on resetting his ratchet wrench.

"Yeah. That's it," I said, catching on. "You're the brains of the family."

"Shhh."

"*Brains* is a dirty word?"

Another shrug.

"Where did you go to school?"

"MIT," he muttered.

"What happened?"

"That's a long story."

"Give me the short version."

"Ran outta dough."

I glanced at his gleaming Harley. "That hog of yours would pay for a couple of semesters."

He looked up from my bike and fixed his disconcerting blue gaze on me. "You don't recognize me, do you?"

I stared.

"Archie Hammond. Paper boy?"

Ohmygod.

He smiled. "I recognized you right away. For a kid, I had a man-sized crush on you."

Archie Hammond. It all came back. The scrawny kid down the street who delivered our paper. He was fourteen when I was seventeen. He used to hang around our front porch on long summer evenings. If it was hot, I'd give him a Coke. And if I was really bored

I'd even shoot the breeze with him or play gin rummy. He was smart for his age. Then I went off to college and never saw him again. Later, Dad told me, "You know that kid, Archie, from down the street? Turns out he won a scholarship to MIT!" And still later, "That kid, Archie—you remember him—he got into some bad trouble and had to drop out of school. His parents are taking it hard."

"Now you remember," he interrupted my reverie. "Local boy makes good. Local boy makes bad. End of story."

"I'm sorry I didn't recognize you, Archie—"

"Pi. That name went in the Dumpster years ago."

"Pi. But you're so different . . ."

"Bodybuilding does wonders." He flexed his biceps.

"Not just that. Your whole . . ." I couldn't find the word.

"Persona?" His eyes twinkled. "Yeah. I can see how you might have been fooled. I was quite a wimp in those days."

"No, you were a nice kid—"

"As for you—your persona was forever etched on my boyish brain. First loves don't erase easily."

I was beginning to feel uncomfortable. When I knew Archie, there was a three-year gap in our ages—an ocean, when you're still in school—eliminating the possibility of any relationship, other than casual friendship. Time had a way of narrowing such gaps. "So, why did you drop out of college?" I asked.

He blinked, as if splashed with cold water, and returned to my bike. I knew our conversation was over.

CHAPTER 6

As I watched Pi put my bike back together, I couldn't help thinking about Archie. What had happened to him? Could he possibly still be buried under that mass of muscle and tattoos? He worked with incredible skill and speed. I liked to watch skilled people work with their hands. My dad had been skilled with his printing tools until everything went electronic: he would set type, fix the presses, prepare the press for a run, with incredible dexterity. And, of course, I never tired of watching the surgeons' hands when I was in training.

Pi stood up and stretched. His hands were coated with black, oily grease. "Boogie, boogie, boogie!" He wiggled his fingers at me.

I cringed, laughing.

"Have you got a hose in this godforsaken hole?"

"You're speaking of my home." I feigned indignation.

His eyes widened. "You *live* in this dump?"

"I provide medical services to the guests of this motel and others in the area. It's convenient to live on-site."

"A motel doctor!" He cut through the shit.

No matter in what fancy terms I couched my occupation, it always came down to that. I nodded.

"What d'ya know. And I thought you were headed for the big-time hospitals. Columbia or Cornell."

I winced. "Things happen. . . ." I said, feebly.

"Don't they, though," he agreed with complete understanding. "But, you're still an M.D., right?"

I nodded.

"Would you take a look at this rash on my tummy?" He jerked up his tattered, grease-stained T-shirt, revealing a few pimples—probably poison ivy.

"If you want my professional opinion, you can come to my office," I said stiffly, pulling a card from my pocket.

"Oh, hoity-toity! Is that my reward for a morning's work?" He gave my newly rehabbed bike a slap.

"I'm sorry. No, I really appreciate—"

"Forget it." He scanned the card

"Yo, Pi. Give me a hand!" a biker hailed him from across the parking lot.

He pocketed the card. "See you at two," and with a wink he took off.

These bikers might be a law unto themselves, but they sure jumped when one of their own barked. Pi had barely left when a hog rumbled up beside me, spraying me with dust and gravel.

"Watch it!" I raised my hand to shield my eyes.

The rider switched off his motor and pushed his goggles up. Red Beard, alias Jingles. "Aw, look at the little trikey. Did Daddy let you take the training wheels off today?"

I moved away. I wished they would leave. The thing that had drawn me to Bayfield was its tranquillity. The bikers had destroyed that. And finding out that their leader was a former neighbor had shaken me more than I realized.

While I was watching Archie—er—Pi, work on my bike, my mind had been totally absorbed, but now fatigue took over and I could barely drag myself up the stairs to my room. When I got inside, I tried to put the whole bizarre morning out of my mind. I called the hospital. Bobby Shoemaker was still comatose. This news was no surprise; my cell phone had been silent during the entire bike rehab. I checked my other messages. Two. One from Dad, one from

Tom. Dad wondering when I was coming for a visit. Tom wondering what night I would be free, *not* on call.

"Not tonight, buster," I spoke into Tom's answering machine. "Tonight I'm hitting the hay at seven o'clock." I looked at my watch and groaned. One-oh-five. In less than an hour I had to be in the office. Dad would have to wait. I set the alarm and fell onto my futon.

I blinked in the bright sun. If anything, my short nap had made me feel worse. As I headed for the office, I passed my bike—and stopped dead. Not only was it a cool forest green, but it had a sleek silver trim. It glittered in the sun like a newly decorated Christmas tree. I walked all around it, staring, pop-eyed. The headlight and taillights gleamed. Maybe their beams would even be visible at night.

"Nice, huh?"

I turned. Pi, too, had undergone a transformation. He wasn't exactly clean, but all traces of his morning work were gone. His hands were greaseless and he was wearing a different tattered T-shirt.

"Why aren't you in your office?" He glanced at his watch—a disk the size of a poker chip bearing a giant face of Popeye.

"I was on my way till I saw this." I waved at my bike. "It's fantastic!"

"Soap and water are great inventions."

"How would you know?"

"Let's go. You're keeping your patient waiting."

"What patient?"

He spread his arms and made a slight bow.

I was reminded that he'd been to a prestigious northeast school.

He followed me into the office. The crowd hadn't arrived yet. (Ha. Ha.) I left him in the waiting room while I dug up some calamine lotion. I brought the bottle out to him.

His face fell. "No examination?"

"Nope. No charge, either."

"Gee. I'd be glad to pay—"

"Sorry. I only give exams on Mondays."

"I'll be back," he promised, stuffing the little pink bottle in the pocket of his jeans.

And I was sure he would. The shy, yearning paper boy I remembered was long gone, I reflected.

A few patients trickled in, and I managed to keep my eyes open until four o'clock. While they were still open I decided to go to the hospital and check on Bobby. When I left the parking lot and hit the road, I went into a state of shock. Was this the same bike I'd been riding for the past six months? It floated rather than rode. And—sniff, sniff—it smelled as sweet as a country breeze. I inhaled deeply and turned up the throttle. Heady stuff, riding a recently rehabbed bike on a May afternoon in south Jersey. Right that minute there was absolutely nothing I'd rather be doing and nowhere I'd rather be. I'd have to think of some way to repay Pi.

This mood quickly evaporated in the hospital parking lot when the young driver who had hit Bobby came rushing up. Had he been lying in wait for me?

"Any news, Doctor?"

"I just got here. But I called in about an hour ago and there was no change."

His face, already gray, turned a shade grayer.

"What's your name?"

"Chris Connor."

"Come on, Chris; let's find out." I stashed my helmet and grabbed my kit.

Together we headed for the entrance.

CHAPTER 7

As we crossed the lobby, a young woman came toward us.

"Any news, Chris?" Her face was pale and strained.

He shook his head. "My wife, Ruth. Dr. Banks."

We shook hands.

"A sad business," I said for something to say, and I guided them to the elevator. Neither answered. The sadness was etched in their faces. Yesterday they had been any young couple, wondering whether to buy a new sofa or have the house painted. Today they were sick with worry over a youngster they had never met and fearful of a lawsuit or even a manslaughter charge. We rode in silence. The doors slid open, revealing another couple, seated on a bench. Bobby's parents.

I nodded a greeting. Instead of rising to meet me and asking after their son, they remained seated in stony silence, oozing dark resentment toward my companions. Although there was plenty of room on the bench, it didn't seem sensible to leave these two couples in such close proximity. I ushered the Connors down the hall to a secret nook I used sometimes to catch my breath during especially difficult cases. Their gratitude was pathetic. I reprimanded myself for feeling more sympathy for these two than for the boy's parents. But the Connors seemed more sincerely concerned about the boy than the Shoemakers, who seemed merely inconvenienced. And I couldn't help holding Bobby's parents partly responsible for the accident. They should have known the where-abouts of their twelve-year-old son at nine o'clock at night. And his bike should have been equipped, if not with lights, at least with reflectors. I couldn't help comparing them to the parents of Sophie, whom I had lost due to a misdiagnosis. The intensity of their anxiety had been excruciating. I shut my eyes to block out the memory.

It was a relief to enter the ICU, where people were unconscious or at least immobile.

"Doctor," the nurse in charge said as she came toward me, "there's been some progress. His vital signs are stronger and Ms. Hamilton said she saw his eyelids flutter."

I pulled Bobby's chart hanging at the end of his bed. His blood pressure was in a normal range and his pulse was regular. The boy lay sleeping. His breathing was even and his face had gained some color. I tried to dampen my rising hopes. In such cases there were often ups and downs before the final outcome was known. "Continue the intravenous and round-the-clock supervision," I said. "Has the surgeon been in?"

"Yes. Here's his report." She grabbed a sheet of paper from a pile. *Vital signs stable. Continue treatment as prescribed.*

"Thanks. I'll be in later tonight. If there's any change, you have my cell phone number."

"Yes, Doctor."

I hastened into the corridor with my news, cautioning myself against raising false hopes. I forced myself to speak to the Shoemak-ers first. They listened to my report in silence. When I had finished, the mother heaved a deep sigh—of relief or exasperation, I wasn't sure. The father slouched back on the bench and shook out his newspaper. No questions. No thanks. No nothing.

The reaction of the Connors was different. Chris allowed him-self the trace of a smile. Tears glistened in Ruth's eyes. Although I knew part of their relief was for themselves, I honestly felt that a major part was for the boy.

. . .

On the way home I decided to stop at the Blue Arrow for a bite. As I dismounted, a shout stopped me. Tom came up. "God, you look shot."

"Thanks."

"Have you been to bed at all?"

"Not really."

His glance wandered to my bike and his expression changed. "What have we here?"

"Like it?"

"What happened?"

"One of those bikers did it. He just took it on himself to—"

"Which one?"

"Archie—Pi. What's the difference? It turns out he was an old neighbor of mine."

"How old?"

"Fourteen when I knew him."

"But I'll bet he's a big boy now."

Did I detect the little green man raising his ugly head? "What of it?"

His face flushed. "Watch yourself, Jo."

"I can handle this," I said stiffly.

Lengthy pause.

"Have you eaten?" I asked finally.

He gave a curt nod.

"Well, I guess I'll just have to eat alone."

He shrugged and walked back to his pickup.

I watched him charge into the road, narrowly missing an SUV. *Shit.* I'd lost my appetite. I remounted my bike. *Men!* I gave the throttle a vicious twist. *What a wonderful world it would be without them.* With this grim reflection I rode back to the motel.

The lobby was blissfully empty. I was surprised to see Maggie at the front desk.

"Early adjournment?" I asked

She nodded. "The prosecution wanted time to track down some documents." She seemed distant and her mouth was set in a thin line.

"Something wrong?" I hoped nothing bad had happened at court.

"I hear you've been fraternizing with the guests," she blurted.

"Where did you hear that?" I snapped. Silly question. The whole staff, from the chambermaids to the trash collectors, must have witnessed my dalliance with Pi.

"Be careful, Jo." Concern had replaced irritation.

"Sure." Why was everyone so worried about my welfare all of a sudden? I made a quick exit.

The silence pervading the motel was palatable. Marie, one of the chambermaids, also my patient and friend, enlightened me. "It's such a nice night, those goons took off for Wildwood," she told me.

A popular seaside watering hole for the wilder set. "Thank god!" I headed eagerly for my room—and oblivion.

But as I neared my door, I heard an unwelcome sound. Music was booming on the other side. Music not to my taste. "Oh, no," I groaned. Only one person I knew had a taste for hard rock—*and* a key to my room. Reluctantly I opened the door.

"Hi, Jo." Becca, my thirteen-year-old-going-on-thirty friend, raised her russet head to look at me. She had made a nest of my bed. It was littered with potato chips, schoolbooks, a Coke precariously balanced on a binder, discarded socks and sneakers. A few months ago, Becca's family had been involved in the illegal smuggling of immigrants in Bayfield—the case in which Maggie's son was now being tried. During that time, I had offered Becca the sanctuary of my room. Although her family had regained its stability, more or less, she still dropped by now and then. "Hi," I croaked.

"You don't seem very glad to see me." She pouted.

"I'm sorry." I forced a smile "It's just that I've been up for twenty-four hours and I was looking forward to some sleep." Becca and I never lied to each other.

"Well, you won't get any here."

For a minute I thought she was being fresh, but she went on, "your neighbors have been having a fight."

Neighbors? Oh, yeah. Vaguely I remembered that obnoxious couple from the lobby was registered in the room next to mine.

"When I came in, the woman was screeching about how she'd choose her own friends and why didn't he mind his own business. Then I think she threw something. There was this awful crash. More screeching of four-letter words. Then the door banged shut. I peeked out and I saw this little man slink off down the hall. I haven't heard anything since."

"How could you hear anything over that racket?" I crossed the room and snapped off the CD player.

"The fight was *before* I put the CD in," she explained patiently.

"So, to what do I owe this visit?"

"I have to write a paper on *Othello* and I need help. *Please*, Jo."

Becca was an orphan. Ema Sheffield, her guardian and aunt, was a practicing poet. But when it came to helping with homework she was a total loss. "Because of my vast knowledge of Shakespeare?" I asked.

"No. Your vast knowledge of life."

Becca always knew how to get around me. "You're kidding."

"Nope. You're a doctor. You've lived in the coolest city in the world. You've had lots of lovers—"

"Wait a minute—"

"You must know something about jealousy. . . ." She grinned mischievously.

"You imp!" I went for her, but she rolled off the bed and pulled a chair between herself and me.

I sighed. "What's the assignment?"

"A five-page essay showing what drove Othello to murder Desdemona."

"Is *that* all?"

She nodded. Sarcasm slid off Becca like waxed soles on a wet deck.

"I don't know why she needs a whole essay on it. I could give her the answer in one word," Becca grumbled.

"Oh?"

"Iago."

"Hmm. Don't you think the seed was already in Othello's head, and Iago just helped it grow?"

"Maybe." Becca was thoughtful. "But if it weren't for that bastard, Othello and Des would probably have lived happily ever after."

"Have you read the whole play?"

"Of course." She was indignant.

"When's it due?"

"Yesterday,"

Naturally.

"But she gave me a one-day extension."

"Let's see it," I said wearily. Fortunately, *Othello* was one of the plays I had read in Shakespeare 101.

She tossed a battered paperback of the play at me and cleared some of her things off my bed to make room for me. "While you're reading, I'll make you some coffee, she offered."

I curled up on the bed and began to read.

Enter Iago and Roderigo

RODERIGO;

Tush, never tell me! I take it much unkindly that thou, Iago,
who hast my purse
As if the strings were thine. . . .

Why couldn't Will write in plain English? Yawning, I forced my gaze back to the page.

When I had scanned the play and we had roughed out an outline for the essay, Becca said, "How's Bobby?"

I blinked. "You know him?" Then I remembered that everyone knows everyone in Bayfield.

"He's two classes below me," she explained. "Everybody at school had to sign his get-well card."

"He's holding his own," I said carefully.

"Meaning?"

"Meaning, he's no better and no worse than after the accident."

She thought about this. "What are his chances?"

"Fifty-fifty." As I said, Becca and I didn't lie to each other.

She was quiet; then she spoke. "His parents are assholes."

I looked at her.

"They have six kids. They don't feed them right. Their lunches are crackers or a candy bar. And their clothes don't fit. They're either too big or too small. Mom and Dad are too busy slurping beer to bother."

"Hmm."

She started to pack up her things. "Can I see him?"

"Not yet. He's in the ICU. But when he goes to a room I'll let you know."

"When . . . or if?"

"If."

She slung her backpack over her shoulder and with one hand on the doorknob turned. "Thanks, Jo."

"Your friendly Shakespeare scholar always at your service."

"I'll let you know what I get."

"If it's less than an A I don't want to hear about it."

"Hey, this teacher's tough!"

"That's what they all say." I waved her out.

Now that I had peace and quiet, I lay wide awake, staring at the ceiling—my thoughts spinning from Bobby, to Bobby's parents, to Pi, to Tom.

WEDNESDAY

CHAPTER 8

Avoiding the lobby and its colorful inhabitants, I rode to the Blue Arrow for breakfast. Subconsciously I guess I was hoping I'd run into Tom again and we could patch up yesterday's misunderstanding. I was surprised he hadn't called. But he was nowhere in sight. My scrambled eggs and hash browns were less tasty without him. From there I headed for the hospital to check on Bobby. On the way, I decided it was time to have a heart-to-heart with his parents about bicycle safety—among other things.

I took a shortcut through the ER. It was as silent as a tomb. Not a happy comparison. But ERs tend to fluctuate from tomblike to circuslike—it's the nature of the beast. It was so churchlike (better simile) I found myself almost tiptoeing to the elevators. And when Bobby's neurosurgeon spoke to me in a normal voice, I jumped.

"Sorry." He smiled. "I didn't mean to startle you."

"No problem." I blushed. Dr. Peters was almost as old as my father, and I felt shy around him.

"Glad I ran into you. I was going to call you. Our patient has regained consciousness."

I wanted to hug the man right there in the corridor. Restraining myself, I said, "That's great news!"

"Are you going to see him now?"

I nodded.

"You'll be pleasantly surprised."

"Thank you, Doctor." I punched the elevator button with renewed vigor.

When I came in, the ICU seemed electrically charged. The nurses were smiling at each other, and when they spied me, their smiles grew broader. One of them hurried over. "You've heard?"

"Yes. I ran into Doctor Peters." I went to Bobby's bed.

The boy was sitting up, eating a bowl of cereal. As I stared, he gave me a crooked grin.

"Hi," I said. "I'm Dr. Banks."

"Hi."

"You're looking good today." I moved around to the side of the bed. "How do you feel?"

"OK."

"Headache?"

"A little." He put his spoon down and touched the injured side of his head.

I examined the stitches. They looked fine and would be absorbed in a little while. "What about the rest of you? Any aches or pains?"

"I've got a big bruise." He rolled down the top of his pajama pants an inch to show me.

"Wow! Every color of the rainbow. But that's nothing. We didn't find any broken bones when we X-rayed you. That's the important thing."

"Except my head," he said.

"Your head isn't a bone."

"Yeah, it is. My pa calls me Bonehead when I do something dumb."

"I see."

"How long was I out?"

"Two days."

"I missed some school."

"Don't worry. You'll make it up easily." The next question most kids would ask was, "When can I go home?" Bobby didn't.

"A friend was asking about you," I told him.

He had gone back to his cereal but looked up with interest.

"Becca Borovy."

The crooked smile returned.

"She'd like to come see you when you're out of here and in a room."

"Cool."

I listened to his chest, made some notations on his chart, and left.

Bobby's parents were not in the corridor or the visitors' lounge. Neither were the Connors. I called both couples on my cell phone and gave them the good news. As expected, the parents' reaction was subdued; the Connors', jubilant. I shook my head all the way to the parking lot. My heart-to-heart would have to wait until Bobby was out of the ICU. I'd be damned if I'd wait around until the Shoe-makers decided to show up.

For the first time, I noticed it was a beautiful day. Wednesday was my official day off. I decided to take a ride. A ride through the coun-tryside—on my new bike—with no special purpose or destination. Just for the fun of it—just for me. I gave the throttle a twist, revved the motor, and took off in the general direction of the bay. I could already smell the salt marshes mixed with the fresh odor of newly turned fields.

The temperature had dropped overnight—from the eighties to the seventies. The air felt cool against my arms and face. My newly rehabbed bike floated between the green fields like a boat on waves. At the end of the road I glimpsed the sparkling bay. When I neared the water's edge I had to remind myself that my bike wasn't amphibious. Braking sharply, I startled a blue heron. It soared above the tall grasses. I soared with it.

"Bobby made it!" I shouted at the bay.

It was almost noon when I returned to the motel. There wasn't a biker in sight. Maybe they had also realized it was a nice day for a run. Paul was at the desk. He waved me over. "Maggie left this for you." He handed me a slip of paper.

"Where is she?"

He shrugged. As usual, in complete denial, Paul pretended he didn't know where his wife went every day or that he had a son on trial. "Look at this." He pointed to a map he was poring over in an old book. "Did you know that part of the state of Delaware is in New Jersey?"

I shook my head, opening the note.

" 'In colonial times, King James the Second of England made a land grant to the Duke of York in New Castle, Delaware,' " he read, running his finger under the type. "The property lines crossed the river and took in part of New Jersey's marshlands," he said, "just a few miles down the road from here—off Snakeskin. Would you believe, those lines still stand today?"★

"Huh." I was only half-listening. I was reading Maggie's note. *Come to the Courthouse if you can. Important.*

She knew Wednesday was my day off. I had half-planned to take in the trial that afternoon anyway. There was only one problem. "Damn," I said.

"Something wrong?" Paul glanced up from the map.

"Yeah. Big-time."

He looked concerned.

"I have to wear a skirt."

"Oh, no. Not that!" He slapped his forehead.

"I knew you'd understand."

★This is a historic fact.

CHAPTER 9

The trial was recessing as I arrived. The front steps were crowded with Bayfielders puffing greedily at long-denied cigarettes and the corriders were filled with people making hurried plans for lunch. I scanned the crowd for Maggie. She spotted me first, tagging me on the shoulder from behind.

"Thanks for coming," she said with feeling.

"I was planning to come anyway."

"Have you eaten?"

I shook my head.

"There's a pizza place around the corner that's fast."

Although I wasn't hungry, I allowed myself to be led.

When we were settled in a corner booth with two slices of pizza and Cokes, Maggie finally told me what was on her mind. "I want you to see Nick."

I sat up. "What?"

"I want you to see how he's changed."

"But I didn't know him *before*," I protested.

She was ready for that. She said, "You're a good judge of character, Jo. You've seen a lot of patients. You've had broad experience with human nature. You can tell if Nick's sincere. You have the instinct."

This was the second time in two days that my "broad experience" had been called upon. First Becca, now Maggie. Didn't they realize that anyone outside of Bayfield has had "broad experience" compared to them? "I don't know . . ." I resisted.

"Please."

I glanced at her tired, anxious face and remembered how she had helped me when I'd first come to Bayfield. Eight months ago I'd turned up out of nowhere in a blue funk. If Maggie and Paul hadn't taken me in, I might have had a full-blown depression. Gone over the brink. Their kindness had saved me. "OK," I said.

"Thanks, Jo." She hadn't touched her pizza. Now she took a big bite and wolfed down the rest in a few minutes. I, on the other hand, nibbled at mine like a refined lady at a high-society tea.

Using her cell phone, Maggie called her lawyer. He made the arrangements for my meeting with Nick. It would probably take place during the afternoon recess, she told me.

Goody.

As we made our way through the crowd returning to the courtroom, my stomach felt queasy, and it wasn't from the pizza. I really didn't want to meet this slime bag. He had exploited helpless immigrants, probably even murdered some of them, and had treated his parents like shit—allowing them to think he was dead and mourn him while he was happily consuming cocaine and heroin in Philadelphia. And now, in an effort to get a lighter sentence, he was playing on the sympathies of the public, the jury, and his mother, by pulling this "born again" crap. What the hell was I going to say to him?

But I knew why Maggie had asked me to see him. She desperately needed one other person to confirm what she felt in her heart. Someone to verify her opinion. Her husband, Paul, was no help. He had shut her out. Refused to have anything to do with their son. She was alone. She needed someone. And I was elected. But I couldn't lie to her. I was prepared to tell her the truth. If necessary, I was ready to inform her that her son was a piece of shit.

As I tried to concentrate on the trial, people kept bumping into one another inside my head as if vying for space in a crowded subway car. Maggie and Nick. Tom and Pi. Bobby and his parents. I wished they'd all clear out at the next stop and leave me alone.

At three-thirty the court recessed and Maggie guided me to the anteroom where my tête-à-tête with her son was to take place. I was looking forward to this like a sheep to the slaughter. Steeling myself, I entered the room. It was small and stuffy, furnished with two straight-backed chairs separated by a long table. A guard stood inside the door on my side of the table. Another guard stood by another door on the other side. As I took my seat, the door on the other side opened and Nick Nelson was ushered in.

CHAPTER 10

Nick's demeanor, as he faced me across the counter, was calm and grave. If I hadn't known his background I might have mistaken him for a young philosophy teacher or a clergyman. What a joke. After I introduced myself, he said, "Thanks for coming."

"I'm here for one reason." I wanted to set things straight right away. "Your mother asked me to come."

He nodded. "I understand."

"What's this about being 'born again'?" I went right to the point. I hadn't come to make small talk.

"That's what some people call it."

"What do you call it?"

He thought a minute. "Renewal . . . reaffirmation . . . restoration."

Pretty highfalutin' stuff from a high school grad turned junkie. A niggling doubt flickered at the rim of my mind. "Tell me about it."

"It happened the second week I was here. Christ came to the foot of my cot—and spoke to me."

With an effort I controlled my facial muscles. "What did He say?"

" 'Rise and follow me.' "

I glanced at the locked doors and two guards. "Somewhat difficult under the circumstances."

A glimmer of a smile. Born-agains are notorious for no sense of humor. He didn't fit the mold. I thawed a little, allowing myself the shadow of an answering smile.

Misinterpreting it, he frowned. "I didn't expect you to believe me," he said. "But I have something to show you." He reached under his tunic and the guard was on him like a shot. He grabbed the neatly folded paper from Nick's hand and examined it carefully. He looked puzzled. Leaning past me, he showed it to the other guard. The second guard shrugged and handed it to me.

It was a delicately rendered portrait of Jesus Christ.

"Where did you get this?" I asked.

"I drew it—right after He left."

Sure you did. And I'm Joan of Arc. It was a remarkable drawing. To my inexperienced eye, at least, it resembled a Dürer or an Inge. "Well, what does that prove?" I clung to my skepticism with an iron fist. "You've seen plenty of pictures of Jesus in museums, art books, the Bible, Sunday school—"

"I've never been to a museum or looked at art books. Our Bible didn't have pictures and there was only one picture of Jesus in Sunday school. It was brown and faded."

I continued to study the drawing. "You're an excellent artist," I said. "Did you take art lessons in school?"

He shook his head. "I was no good at art. They switched me to shop—where I could hammer and saw. I'm good at that."

"Well, where *did* you learn to draw like this?"

"I don't *know* how to draw like this."

"But . . ."

"I drew this right after He left. I haven't been able to draw anything since."

"Have you tried?"

He nodded and made a zero with his thumb and finger. "Zilch."

He couldn't have found this drawing in the prison. They had a library, but this wasn't from a printed book. It was an original drawing made in pencil on a sheet of paper torn from a sketch pad. And it looked as if the paper had been torn off hastily; the tear across the top was ragged. And he couldn't have brought it into the prison with him. They always stripped the prisoners and confiscated everything they owned. He must have drawn it himself. There was no other explanation. But under the influence of what? A vision? Hallucination, more likely. But he had been detoxed months ago, when he first came in. Still, those drugs sometimes had lasting effects. They did strange things to the brain. I took another tack. "Where did you get the pencil and paper?" I doubted if they provided prisoners with art supplies.

His answer was so low I had to lean forward to hear it. "I stole them."

Ah, now we were getting somewhere. That I could believe.

"We have a rec time when they let us draw or paint. I stole this pencil stub and a sheet of paper."

"Why?"

His brow creased. "I don't know. I just had this strong feeling I might need them."

Oh, boy. At least he didn't say voices told him to do it. "Are you telling me Jesus suggested that you steal?"

He lowered his eyes. When he raised them again, they were angry. "I didn't expect you to believe me." He drew a deep breath and his voice rose. "Listen, I don't care what you think. And I don't want any favors from you. I don't expect any. All I want . . . is to make it up with my parents. That's all I care about."

I stared at him. "Don't you think it's a little late for that?"

He stared back. "I don't know."

"Time's up." The guard on Nick's side came forward.

I rose. As I left Nick, his expression was no longer angry. It was weary—and blank. Remembering all the suffering he had caused, I felt no sympathy for him.

When I came out, Maggie was nowhere in sight. The trial must have resumed. I knew I should go back in, but I couldn't face her. Not now. I felt drained. I went back to the motel. Giving the lobby a wide berth, I went straight to my room. I would talk to Maggie tonight—or, even better, tomorrow.

. . .

Around six o'clock, I made a big mistake. I went down to the lobby to pick up my mail. Maggie was there.

"What happened to you, Jo? I looked all over for you."

"Sorry. I was tired. I came back here."

Casting me a reproachful look, she grabbed my arm and led me over to the sofa. As soon as we were seated, she said, "Well, what did you think?"

A bunch of rowdy bikers burst into the lobby. Maggie frowned. They made quite a rumpus around the vending machine. Each left with a soda. Maggie turned back to me. "Did he show you the picture?"

Reluctantly I nodded.

Still clasping my arm, she asked, "What did you think?"

"It's beautifully done," I said feebly.

"It is, isn't it. Every hair in place. It looks right out of a museum."

"Hmm." Avoiding her gaze, I asked, "Did Nick draw a lot as a kid?"

"Never."

"Did he take art at school?" Not that I doubted the word of her irreproachable son.

Maggie shook her head, "In fact, he did so poorly in art— couldn't draw anything but stick figures—they transferred him to shop, where he did much better. He made me the most beautiful birdhouse."

"What about after he left home? Did he take any courses?"

Maggie looked at me. We both knew the kind of courses he had taken.

I sighed. "Beats me," I said.

"Don't you think . . ." Maggie spoke hesitantly, ". . . that maybe what he told us might be true?"

I refused to meet her gaze. When it came down to it, I couldn't tell her the truth. What I really thought: drugs had damaged his neurological system so badly that he now hallucinated without their help.

"Yo, Jo!"

I looked up. Pi was hailing me from across the lobby. For the first time, I was glad to see a biker. As he ambled toward me, Maggie pointedly excused herself. I felt like a louse, but what could I do?

CHAPTER 11

I was feeling so lousy I let Pi talk me into a beer. He pulled a couple of cans from his backpack right there in the lobby. I glanced at the front desk. Maggie seemed to be absorbed in a romance novel.

"Not here," I snapped.

He raised an eyebrow.

"No drinking in the lobby. It's a rule."

"Rules," he grumbled as I led him out to the parking lot, "are meant to be broken." This was followed by a long rant on freedom, independence, and the Bill of Rights. Apparently bikers like to bullshit about this stuff.

I settled us on a bench at a battered picnic table reserved for guests. When we'd finished the beers, he pulled out two more—they were even frosty. I refused to question this miracle. While he continued to rant, I noticed Sunny talking animatedly to the female half of the only nonbikers at the motel. He seemed to be trying to convince her to go for a ride. She was listening intently, her head cocked at a perky angle. Her wimpy husband was nowhere in sight. When I looked again they were gone.

While I listened to two beers' worth of Pi's biker bullshit, I kept searching for vestiges of the younger Archie, to no avail. Reconciling myself to the present Pi, I interrupted him. "What do you think about this born-again thing?"

His reaction surprised me. Instead of a horselaugh, I was greeted with silence. It wasn't a long silence, but when it came in the middle of an animated rant, it seemed long.

"Why?" he asked.

"I know this guy—a real scumbag. He's in prison now and all of a sudden he claims he's been reborn, transformed . . . sees visions. I think they're drug induced myself and he's hallucinating."

Pi grinned. "So now you're a substance abuse expert."

I frowned. "He's not a patient. He's the son of a friend of mine and he's put her through the meat grinder. I don't want him to do it again."

"She believes him?"

"Of course. He's her son. Her one and only baby boy. Adopted, though."

"What's he done?"

"Oh, nothing much. Pretended to be dead for three years while she and his father mourned him. Then he showed up as the foreman of a slave camp full of immigrants. May have even bumped off a few—"

"Oh, *that* scumbag. I've been following his story in the papers."

I told him about my visit with Nick—and the picture.

No response.

"You're a big help." I started to get up.

"No. Wait." He put a hand on my arm. "I knew a case like this once. Piggy Sylvester. And I was just like you. Bullshit, I thought. I wouldn't have anything to do with the motherfucker. He was the worst kind of scumbag. A snitch. The kind you'd dismember limb by limb if you got your hands on him. If he hadn't been arrested we would have done just that—believe me. . . ."

"But . . . ?"

"He went to jail. And he claimed all that shit you're talkin' about. A new man. Washed clean. Born again, blah, blah, blah. Well, they locked him up for three years. I totally forgot about him. So did everybody else. Then, one day, down in Arkansas, I saw this poster: BORN AGAIN BIKE RALLY. With a date and a place. The place was a campground on the outskirts of town—and the name of the preacher, in two-foot-high letters, was PIGGY SYLVESTER! Well, I had to see this. I couldn't leave town. I waited around the two extra days and barreled out to that place on one wheel, half-intending to kill the lyin', cheatin' bastard. . . ."

"But . . ."

"There was this sort of impromptu stage set up—with flood-lights—and a tape playin' some crazy mix of country and gospel. And, my god, there must have been a thousand bikers out there. I'd watched them coming into town, of course, during that two-day wait, but seeing them all together . . . was something else! I didn't recognize any of them. But they looked the same as any other biker group: tattoos, piercings—"

"Did they smell the same?"

He ignored that. "They were sittin' and lyin' on the ground. There was only one difference. No smoke, no pot, and no booze. A real sober crowd. Just hangin' out, bullshitting among themselves. All of a sudden there was dead silence. I looked up at the stage, and there was Piggy. He was standing there all decked out in a white robe, arms raised above his head. As I stared, with a flick of his hands he signaled for everyone to stand. And, would you believe, all those motherfuckers rose—as one—as if he had them tied to an invisible string." Pi stared at his beer as if he could see Piggy reflected in the top of the can. "Then Piggy shouts in this unbelievable voice, *'Praise the Lord!'* And those thousand bikers shouted back, *'Praise the Lord!'* It scared the shit out of me."

"What happened next?"

"Piggy signaled for them to all sit down. They sat. Then he went into his spiel."

"What did you do?"

"I left. But . . . I gotta tell you . . ." Pi said, fixing his eyes on mine, "there was something about him. If I hadn't gotten out of there . . . he would have had me. Even though I *knew* he was a snitch—a real scumbag."

"Great. So what are you telling me? I should pay attention to Nick?" I was really fed up.

"Hell, I don't know what you should do. I'm just telling you what happened to me."

"Well, thanks." I stood up.

"Hey, wait. . . ."

As I sought out my bike, I passed Sunny and Fran. They had just come back from their ride. Fran was cozily cuddled up to Sunny's backside, her arms around his waist, and Sunny looked like the cat that swallowed the canary. Stan suddenly emerged between two parked cars. "Where've you been, Honey?" His tone was reproachful. "I've been looking all over for you."

She eyed him sleepily, as if she wasn't sure who he was. "Oh, Sunny took me for a ride." She lazily extricated herself. As she stood up, she noticed some grease spots on her shorts and her manner changed. "Look at that!" She stared accusingly at Sunny. "I paid an arm and a leg for these at Saks."

Sunny adopted a hangdog expression.

"Easy, Honey," Stan soothed.

Fran turned on him. "You have to buy me a new pair. These stains will never come out."

Sunny wisely took this opportunity to disappear.

I mounted my bike and went for a long ride.

CHAPTER 12

It was a beautiful evening. But the sun setting behind a solitary farmhouse in a field, the pungent smell of the marshes, and the salty taste of the bay—nothing worked its magic on me that night. As I neared the motel, I felt just as rotten as when I'd left.

There was still plenty of light. Daylight savings had been reinstalled a month ago for the benefit of the farmers (although I'd never seen any farmer take advantage of this bonanza). After the stillness of the marshes and the bay, my ears were supersensitive to the slightest noises. As the motel loomed ahead, a strange mix of sounds came to me. Heavy metal music, the revving of bike motors, all punctuated by occasional shrill yips and yodels. As I drew closer, I saw bikes charging in and out of the parking lot, making pointless U-turns. The noise of Black Sabbath was earsplitting. The yips and yodels more frequent.

I slowed to a crawl, intending to cruise by unnoticed and evaluate the situation. But as I neared the entrance a bike cut me off, almost ramming me.

"Asshole!" I yelled. Shaken, I ground to a halt, dismounted, and rolled my bike by hand into the lot. The place was in chaos. The asphalt was littered with empty beer cans and bottles. Bikes were parked every which way. The bikers seemed to have tripled like mushrooms (toadstools, more like it). Guffawing, yelling, pummeling one another, they had taken over the lot. And something new had been added. Women. Where had they come from? They looked just like the men with their piercings, tattoos, and leather, with one exception. Boobs—and they did everything to show them off.

I decided I couldn't leave my bike in its usual spot, unprotected. I would have to stash it somewhere else. But where? Mike's Garage? That would mean a long walk back. Damn. I needed this like a hole in the head. I was still suffering from a sleep deficit and had planned to hit the sack early. I was standing against the wall, holding on to my bike, when Pi approached with a beer in each hand. "You look thirsty." He handed one to me.

It took me only a split second to decide he was right. I drank deeply. Maybe that was my trouble. I was too sober.

"That's better!" he shouted over the din. "Drink up! It's party time."

"This is a party?" I screamed back. "I thought it was a riot!"

"You've obviously never been to a riot,"

"Where did the women come from?"

Before he could answer, Red Beard, alias Jingles, sidled up. He stood out among the other bikers because he was tall and had a long neck. Most of these bikers were stocky and had no necks, like football players. And where the others had muscles that bulged like rocks, Jingles's were smooth and sinewy, like ropes. Ignoring me, he eyed Pi reproachfully and said, "You're not mingling."

The look Pi gave him would have discouraged Osama bin Laden.

"Why ain't you dancing?" Jingles persisted.

"How much is this blowout costing?" Pi's eyelids drooped—a sign, I had come to recognize, of his displeasure.

Jingles shrugged.

"Seriously."

"Not to worry." Jingles grinned and turned to me. "Wanna dance?"

I shook my head.

"Aw, come on." He grabbed my arm.

"Fuck off." Although Pi's voice was barely audible over the racket, it made me jump.

Jingles didn't budge.

I tried to edge away. Pi caught my other arm, his gaze never leaving Jingles. For a minute I felt like that baby in the King Solomon story. Abruptly Jingles let go of me and moved off.

"We picked up the girls in Wildwood," Pi said, answering the question I'd asked light-years ago. He took my empty beer can and squashed it. "Want another?"

Did I? The first one had relaxed me, despite the chaos and the clamor. Maybe a party was what I needed. Maybe that was my trouble. Maybe I was too uptight. Oh, what the hell. "Sure."

He disappeared. I sank back against my bike to enjoy the scene.

CHAPTER 13

Pi was gone a long time. I'd finished my beer and was more than ready for a second. I scanned the melee but didn't see any sign of him. Someone threw a bottle. It shattered on the asphalt. Others followed. Trash cans were kicked and hurled around the lot. Hammerhead shuffled by with a bunch of balloons. He offered me one. I took a pink one. He stood staring at me, as if waiting for something. Was I supposed to pay? I reached into my jeans.

"No, man." He detached a blue balloon from his bouquet, carefully untied the string, and pressed the opening to his mouth. As he inhaled deeply, a beatific smile spread across his face. "See," he said, in a high squeaky voice, completely unlike his own. Light dawned. He was offering me a helium high. The biker's idea of an hors d'oeuvre?

"No, thanks." I tried to give the balloon back.

He shook his head, the remains of the peaceful smile still decorating his face. "Keep it for later!" he squeaked, and moved on.

The noise was escalating, if that was possible. Two bikers were facing off. One held the jagged neck of a broken bottle. The tenor of the party had changed, from a good-natured brawl to something more sinister.

Jack-the-night-clerk stepped out of the motel, stood gaping for a minute, and darted back inside.

The soothing effects of my first beer had worn off. I decided I'd better put an end to this ruckus before they wrecked the motel—my home—or someone got hurt. As I pulled out my cell phone to call 911, someone shoved me, knocking the phone to the ground. Arms like steel girders gripped me from behind, lifted me up, and tossed me over a shoulder made of granite. My bearer lunged through the crowd. The bikers, and their girls, grinned, guffawed, and applauded as I sailed past, ass end in the air.

"Yo, Sunny! Way to go!"

"Find yourself a piece?"

"Gonna share?"

Kicking and screaming, I pounded my fists against my kidnapper's back. It was like hitting a tank with toothpicks. From my awkward position the karate techniques I'd learned to thwart Manhattan muggers were totally useless. Visions of gang rape filled my head. Desperately I searched the crowd for the only one who might come to my aid. Pi was nowhere in sight.

Suddenly, out of the corner of my eye, I glimpsed a pickup truck rolling into the parking lot. The driver jumped out and pulled something from the back.

Tom stood poised, his bow and arrow aimed directly at me. *"Drop her or I'll take your goddamned earring off!"*

For a split second nobody moved. Then everyone began to whoop and holler. I was the only one who took him seriously. Oh, my god, what if he missed?

Zing!

"Ow! He nicked me!" Sunny slapped the side of his head, letting me slide to the ground.

When I looked up I saw blood gushing from his right ear. I leaped up and searched for a pressure point. Finding one, I leaned on it with all my strength.

"You're helping that creep?" Tom was at my side.

"Call nine-one-one!" I ordered.

"What's happening?" Pi appeared out of nowhere.

"Look on the ground for his earlobe," I barked. "It should be easy to find; it has a gold earring in it."

Obediently Tom called 911 on his cell and Pi began searching the lot for the earlobe. The other bikers and their women gawked from a healthy distance.

Pi spotted the earring on a bike seat—glinting in a last ray of sun. Attached to it was a small piece of ragged flesh. Holding it at arm's length, he brought it to me. Funny what a scrap of ear could do to a tough biker. His face, normally ruddy, was the color of vanilla pudding.

"Hang on to it," I said maliciously, "until the ambulance comes." The moans of my patient were getting on my nerves, his garlicky breath was asphyxiating me (I wondered what he'd had for dinner), plus my arms were tiring from applying pressure to keep him from bleeding to death. "What did the nine-one-one operator say?" I asked Tom, who was still hovering at my side.

"Said they'd be out right away."

At first the other bikers had been too drunk and too preoccupied to assimilate what had happened. Slowly they began to catch on. One of their brothers had been dissed, and revenge was the accepted Apostle Code. As they huddled at the other end of the parking lot, their mutual gaze fixed on Tom.

"Get out of here!" I urged him.

"What?"

I nodded at the knot of bikers moving toward him. Some brandished broken bottles; a couple were swinging chains.

"Meet me at Harry's. We have to talk." Tom dashed for his pickup. And none too soon. As he started up, some bikers were scrambling up the back of the truck trying to jump inside. Others mounted their bikes and were revving their motors preparing for pursuit. I prayed he would have the sense to head for the marshes and the secret winding roads that only a native Bayfielder knew.

"It hurts," Sunny moaned. My attention was dragged back to my patient.

"Good," I said. The wail of a siren. "Thank god," I whispered.

Sunny heard it, too, and instantly grew more anxious. "Can they fix it? Will it hurt? Are you coming with me?" he asked.

"Yes. Probably. And no," I answered his questions in order.

"Take it easy," Pi soothed Sunny in a fatherly tone. "They'll have you fixed up in no time."

As the ambulance pulled into the lot, the bikers scattered to make a path for it. Two medics jumped out. One threw open the back doors while the other rushed to relieve me. Expertly he took over, bundling Sunny into the emergency vehicle.

"Give him the lobe!" I urged Pi.

Pi hurried after the medic.

Moments later, they were gone. The parking lot had miraculously emptied. No one was left but me, and . . . Pi.

Once he was relieved of the earlobe, and assured that Sunny was in good hands, Pi's natural color had returned, along with his forceful personality. "What happened?" he demanded. He must have been occupied elsewhere during the incident. Inside, getting me a beer, I guessed.

"Oh, nothing much," I snapped. "Just a little attempted rape by one of your buddies."

Pi scanned me from head to foot. Satisfied that I was still intact, he demanded, "Who shot Sunny's ear off?"

"Earring," I corrected.

"Your boyfriend, right?"

I didn't answer.

Torn by divided loyalties, he seemed unsure how to react—with outrage or humor. Humor won out. His laugh rolled across the parking lot. Still laughing, he leaped on his bike. Before he roared off, he shouted, "I better get to the hospital and make sure those docs don't murder my boy!"

CHAPTER 14

Left to myself, I noted for the first time that the blood from Sunny's wound had soaked the front of my T-shirt and splattered my jeans and boots. Time to get cleaned up.

Back in my room, I washed my white tee in cold water and Clorox and scrubbed my jeans where the red stains were rapidly turning brown. My boots would have to wait until morning, when I could hose them down in the parking lot. All these efforts were probably in vain. I'd probably have to throw out everything but the boots.

While I was performing these domestic chores, I was trying to keep my fear for Tom under control. What if they'd caught up with him? What if . . . I hurriedly pulled on clean clothes.

The bar was dark. As I peered through the murky gloom, anxiety ballooned inside me. I didn't see him. Nothing to do but wait. I slipped into an empty booth, taking the seat facing the door, and ordered a beer. My mind filled with unwelcome images. Tom being dragged from behind the steering wheel, Tom being beaten with chains, Tom . . . slid into the seat across from me. He hadn't come through the door. He had come from behind.

"Where were you?" My relief burst out in irritation.

"The men's."

"What happened?"

"A couple of them followed me, but I lost them in the swamp. I think one of them got stuck in a ditch." Normally he would have laughed, but not tonight.

"Do you think you're safe here?" I scanned the room.

He didn't answer.

"You'd better stay away from the motel until they're gone."

The waitress came to take our order. I asked for another beer.

With growing irritation, I watched him methodically tear matches from a matchbook, making a little pile on the table.

Harry's was a retro kind of place. It still allowed smoking throughout. Tom didn't smoke, but he always carried matches. *A throwback to his Boy Scout days,* I thought snidely. *What's wrong with you?* I gave my head a shake. "Thanks for coming to my aid," I said. "I was a little worried at first, but you're a good shot."

He glanced up from the match mess he had made. "I've been a bowman for twenty years."

Our beers came. He swept the ruined matches aside. We each took a long draft. I knew he was waiting for an explanation. And deserved one. I took a deep breath.

"It happened so fast," I began. "I drove up on my bike and there was this party going on in the parking lot. At first it looked like sort of fun. You know, totally off the wall. Somebody handed me a beer. I guess I had two. But then something changed. They started breaking bottles and hurling trash cans, and . . . I thought of the Nelsons. Neither of them was there. Jack was on duty. He came out of the motel. I think he intended to tell them to stop. But when he saw what was going on, he darted back inside. That's when I decided to call nine-one-one. But Sunny grabbed me—and I dropped my phone."

Tom's hand tightened around his mug.

"If you hadn't come—"

"You would have been fine," he said evenly. "As soon as he put you down, you would have beaten him to a pulp. That's not the point."

"What's the point?" I asked innocently.

"Who was that guy who picked up the earlobe?"

"Pi?" I said, too quickly.

Retrieving the matches, Tom returned to their mutilation.

I traced a design in the frost on my mug. The silence lengthened. I had to say something. "At first I thought all those guys were alike. Grotesques from some horror show—with two brain cells. But . . ."

He waited.

"I was wrong. I mean, there's more to them than you think. You can't stereotype them. Some are manual workers and day laborers. But one's an artist; another's an actor. Pi's a mathematician. But they have this one thing in common—that binds them together. . . ."

He frowned. "What's that?"

"The bike. Not just the physical Harley, but what it stands for. It's a symbol for . . . risk, power, brotherhood—freedom!"

"Violence. Intimidation. Destruction. *Rape!*"

I looked away. "I guess . . ."

The waitress took our empty mugs. Tom ordered two more beers. I stopped him. "Make mine a bourbon." I needed more fortification

"You were telling me about Pi," he prodded.

"He's the leader. He keeps them under control."

"Like tonight?"

Tom rarely indulged in sarcasm. That was my forte. I ignored it.

"The guys worship him."

"And the girls?"

"I don't know. I haven't seen—"

"One particular girl?" He fixed his own not inconsiderable gaze on me.

"Don't be ridiculous." I took a large gulp of bourbon. When I looked up, his expression was hurt. I reached over to squeeze his hand. He pulled away.

"He was at MIT," I said, "and dropped out."

"Terrific. Another point in his favor."

"But he's young and has promise. It's such a waste. Maybe—"

"You can reform him, send him back to school, and someday he'll invent a substitute for the gasoline motor or take us all to Mars."

I didn't respond.

"You have a tendency to want to fix everything, Jo. Be careful. Pi's a big boy now. Not the little paper boy you remember."

"You just can't believe a man and woman can be friends—with no sex—can you?" The bourbon had kicked in.

He looked surprised. "And you can?"

"Of course. I had loads of male friends in med school—"

"I'll bet you did."

Had I heard right? "What?"

"Finish your drink. I'll take you home."

"Don't be sore."

He stood. "Drink up."

I didn't want it. I was confused. What had I said? I couldn't remember. I hadn't meant to make him mad. He had rescued me. My knight in shining armor. As I stood up, my legs wobbled and I almost knocked over my chair. Shit, I was *drunk*. I had eaten and slept very little in the past twenty-four hours, and after such an emotional evening one beer and a couple of swallows of bourbon had sent me to la-la land.

Grabbing my arm, Tom dropped a tip on the table and hurried me out of the bar.

I started for my bike, but he stepped in front of me. "Give me your keys and wait here." He rode my bike over to his truck, yanked down the tailgate, and wrestled the wooden ramp he always carried to the ground. He rolled my bike onto the flatbed. After slamming the tailgate shut, he ordered, "Get in."

I moved toward the cab, using the side of the truck for support, and climbed awkwardly into the passenger seat.

He drove faster than usual—anxious to get rid of me? When we pulled into the parking lot, there was a state police car in front of the motel. *He's after Tom for speeding,* was my first fuzzy thought. A trooper stepped out of the car, hand raised.

Tom braked and called from the window, "What's up, Officer?"

"You'll have to park somewhere else."

Behind the flashing lights I made out two more state police cars and a band of troopers milling around the lot, bearing flashlights. Even in my inebriated state I knew they couldn't *all* be after Tom.

"My passenger lives here," Tom said. "Can I drop her off?"

"What's her name?"

"Jo Banks."

"Dr. Banks?" He came closer and peered in the window.

Oh, god, I hope he doesn't make me take a Breathalyzer test. Hell, I'm not even driving. "Yes," I said.

"Get out. We've been looking for you."

"Wait a minute. What's this all about?" Tom stretched his arm across my chest, preventing me from moving.

"There's been an accident. She's wanted for questioning. What's your name?"

"Canby. Tom."

"Well, what a coincidence, Mr. Canby. You and your girlfriend are both wanted for questioning. We were told Dr. Banks was a near rape victim here tonight, and you may be charged with assault and battery for pulling some van Gogh–like stunt. You'd both better come inside."

"Is that an order?"

"Let's put it this way." The brim of the trooper's hat hid his eyes in shadow as he spoke. "If you don't come voluntarily now, you may be subpoenaed in the morning."

"Who was hurt?" I leaned across Tom.

"Not hurt. Dead," the trooper said. "A biker."

"Which one?"

Tom looked at me.

"I don't know his real name. His buddies called him . . . Sunny."

I sank back against the seat. "How did he die?" I asked more calmly.

"Can't tell you that. You'd better come inside."

As we made our way to the motel entrance, I caught a glimpse of Sunny. His yellow hair splayed in a ragged halo against the tarmac, a wad of white bandage like an earmuff, covering his left ear, and his battered bomber boots pointing at the night sky.

CHAPTER 15

Every light in the lobby was turned on and every seat taken. Not that there were many seats. One couch and two chairs. Bikers stood in clusters talking in hushed—for bikers—tones. I caught a glimpse of Maggie and Paul in their little office talking intently to a stranger. A bald man in a shabby tweed suit, he stood out among the colorful bikers and the gray troopers. The Nelsons' faces were taut and strained. Jack was huddled on a corner of the couch, trying to keep his distance from two burly bikers who had taken over the rest of it.

Coming from the dark, Tom and I stood blinking in the glare. The man in tweeds stepped forward to make an announcement: "You may all go now. But no one may leave Bayfield until further notice."

Since most of the people either were staying at the motel or lived in Bayfield, this announcement had little impact.

"Does that mean us?" Tom asked the trooper hopefully.

He ignored him.

"Who's that man?" I asked.

"Peck—Major Crimes," the trooper said.

As the crowd gradually thinned out, I saw Jingles slide up to Mr. Peck (Jingles never walked; he slid) and say something in his ear. Peck nodded. I had hoped to catch up with Maggie or Paul before they left, but they had disappeared right after Peck's announcement.

Jack had also vanished. Pi was nowhere in sight. Peck came toward us. Tom gripped my arm. "Let me do the talking," he whispered.

I was happy to obey, even though I no longer felt drunk. There's nothing like finding a body on your doorstep to sober you up. Black coffee and cold showers pale in comparison. I wondered what effect—if any—it would have on my hangover the next morning.

"Who's this?" Peck asked the trooper who had us in tow.

The trooper gave our names.

"Thanks, Fred. You can go," Peck said. "I'm Detective Peck, Major Crimes Division." He led us over to the couch that was still occupied by two bikers—Mickey, the comic book artist, and Hash Brown, the short-order cook. "We need this space," the detective told them. To my surprise, the bikers left without a murmur. When we were seated, Peck said, "I just have a few questions."

"I'm sorry, sir, but we're not answering any questions without our lawyer." Tom was polite but firm.

I didn't know we *had* a lawyer, but it sure sounded good.

"Do lawyers work night shifts in Bayfield?" Peck asked with a bemused expression.

Tom didn't answer.

The detective shrugged. "As you wish."

Tom crossed the lobby before taking out his cell phone.

Peck and I sat in silence while Tom made his call. I was completely sober now but feared some lingering alcoholic fumes might leak Peck's way if I opened my mouth.

Tom came back. "He'll be right over," he said.

I wanted to ask who "he" was but thought better of it. If one had a lawyer, one should know his name.

The three of us sat silently, in the now-empty lobby, waiting for the lawyer. Someone had turned off the main light switch, and the only illumination came from a standing lamp (which must have had a twenty-five-watt bulb) and a small desk lamp in the office where Jack had reappeared with a paperback. He glanced our way once. I winked at him, but he didn't respond. It would take Jack a few days to recover from tonight's events, I decided.

With an elaborate yawn, Peck reached for a tattered copy of the *Bayfield Bugle* that lay on a table nearby and began to read. I fiddled with a button on my jeans jacket, until it fell off. Tom was the only one who remained in complete repose. He was good at that. A hunter's knack acquired while waiting for the deer to come out, I supposed.

A gust of damp night air blew into the lobby, followed by a tired man in a rumpled suit. Tom leaped up. "Thanks for coming, Henry."

"No problem." He grinned. "What's going on?"

"This is Henry Wosky," Tom introduced him to Peck.

Before rising to shake the lawyer's hand, Peck carefully folded the newspaper and tucked it neatly in the side of the sofa. Tom pulled up the remaining orange vinyl chair for the lawyer. Since I was supposed to know Wosky, Tom said, "And you know Dr. Banks."

A smart lawyer, Wosky merely nodded.

When everyone was reseated (except me; since I had been seated already), Peck took the floor. "We had an unfortunate incident here tonight. . . ."

At last, I thought, *we're going to find out what happened to Sunny.*

CHAPTER 16

I was pondering the use of the word *incident* to describe the sudden death of a young man when Peck addressed me: "Dr. Banks, I'd like you to give me a full account of what happened here before you left tonight."

Tom sent me a wary glance. I guess he was afraid I was still drunk. But, as Rick said in *Casablanca,* "that was all over long ago." I'd never felt more sober. I gave a clear and concise account of the biker party as I remembered it—from the time I arrived until Sunny left for the hospital. The detective took rapid notes, interrupting me only once—to ask the nature of my relationship to Pi. Sensing Tom's interest in my answer as well as Peck's, I chose my words carefully. "Just an acquaintance. He arrived three days ago. On a whim one afternoon, he rehabbed my bike. We had a few beers afterward. That was it. Oh . . . and he came to my office—briefly."

Tom shot me a look.

"He wanted to consult me about a rash. I diagnosed a mild case of poison ivy and gave him some calamine lotion."

"And where is he now?"

I blinked. *He's missing?* "I have no idea. Have you checked his room?"

He nodded. "When was the last time you saw him?"

"Around eight o'clock. Here, in the parking lot. When he left on his bike I thought he was going to the hospital to see Sunny."

"According to my reports . . ." he took a sheaf of notes from his pocket and consulted them before continuing, "he only stopped at the hospital briefly and no one has seen him since. Do you know what his relationship to Sunny was?"

A scene flashed through my mind. Sunny being tossed out of this very lobby—by Pi. Humiliated in front of all his biker brothers. But I also remembered the Dutch Uncle tone with which Pi had given Sunny a lecture and his obvious concern when Sunny was injured. I shook my head. "All these bikers are very close. They have a deep bond—more than friendship. More like family." I could feel the cold wave of skepticism emanating from Tom on my left. As Peck considered my answer, I couldn't contain myself any longer. "How did Sunny die, Mr. Peck? We need to know . . ." I glanced at Tom, ". . . if his death had anything to do with his earlier injury."

"My clients have a right to this information," Henry Wosky said, backing me up.

"The trouble is—" the detective replied, and scratched his head. "I can't answer you. We don't know. He was treated at the hospital, a surgeon reattached his earlobe, and he was sent home, or rather, back here. They gave him some painkillers to help him sleep and everyone thought he'd gone to bed. But around midnight a couple of bikers pulled into the parking lot and almost ran over him. He was lying flat out on the asphalt. They tried to revive him—without success. Then they called nine-one-one. But the paramedic's efforts failed, too. Finally the state police were called and our ME pronounced him . . ." he paused, ". . . dead."

Death, it seems, gives even a detective pause.

"There were no marks on his body other than the earlier wound inflicted by you." Peck sent Tom a wry look. "They've taken him to the morgue and are doing an autopsy right now. But we won't know anything conclusive until morning."

Tom and I exchanged glances.

"Are my clients murder suspects?" Wosky asked.

The detective, taking pity on us, said, "Judging from the ME's cursory examination, the victim's death was caused by something other than his previous injury."

Together we expelled our tightly held breaths.

"What led him to this conclusion?" Wosky asked.

"A number of things. The nature of his pallor, the clammy touch of his skin, the dilation of his pupils, and especially . . . an odor around his mouth."

"Garlic?" I asked.

He looked at me keenly. "What makes you say that?"

"When I was applying pressure to his wound, our faces were very close and the garlicky odor was overpowering. I remember wondering what he'd had for dinner."

"This is important . . ." Peck said.

We waited for him to go on, but he didn't.

"Since when is garlic a poison, Mr. Peck?" asked Wosky.

"Not garlic," he said softly. "Arsenic. One of the symptoms of acute arsenic poisoning is a strong odor resembling garlic."

The rest of Peck's questions concentrated on our whereabouts after we had left the motel and when we returned. A quick phone call verified that we had been at Harry's the whole time. The bartender and several customers who knew us vouched for us. Peck's interest in Tom's whereabouts before the parking lot party was not great, I noticed. I had the impression that his suspicions were centered on people directly connected to the motel. Guests and employees. He stuffed his notes back in his pocket and let us go. As we were leaving, he called us back. "If you run into that Pi fellow, let me know. I'm anxious to talk to him." He gave Tom his card.

While Tom was thanking Wosky for coming out so late, I gathered my courage and went after the detective. "Why are you so interested in Pi, Mr. Peck?" I asked. "Poison is the last weapon a biker would use on another biker. They're violent, not sneaky."

He looked at me with interest. "You have a point, doctor," he said. "But you see, Pi is the only one who fled the scene. And he has a prison record."

So that was the "trouble" Dad had referred to that had caused Archie to drop out of school. What had he done, I wondered, to warrant imprisonment?

"But don't worry, we're not picking on your friend." He smiled. "We're pursuing other leads as well."

I wondered how Peck had learned about Pi's record so quickly. An image of Jingles whispering to Peck in the lobby earlier came back to me.

When Tom and I stepped out of the motel, there was no trace of Sunny. Only one state trooper remained to guard the crime scene. He sat at the wheel of his car, dozing. A light wind caused the yellow crime tape to ripple.

After unloading my bike, we leaned against Tom's pickup, neither of us speaking. But this time the silence wasn't awkward. Something had been resolved between us back in the motel. The magnitude of recent events had revealed our differences for what they were—petty. He bent and kissed me. I returned his kiss.

"I don't like leaving you here," he said. "Sure you don't want to come back to my place?"

I hesitated—tempted. I didn't relish returning to my empty room. *Sissy*. "I shook my head. "Thanks. I'd better not. I have to be at the hospital early."

We kissed again and he drove off.

CHAPTER 17

Although exhausted, I couldn't sleep. I lay staring into the dark, my thoughts churning like wet laundry in a washing machine. First there was Tom. I was relieved that he didn't seem to be a serious suspect and happy that we had become reconciled. It was sweet of him to ask me back to his place. Very un-PC, but sweet nonetheless.

And then there was Pi. He seemed to be the detective's number one suspect. Pi—a poisoner? The thought of any biker stooping to poison was ludicrous. It wasn't their style. They were boisterous, violent, in-your-face. Not sneaky. But where was he? Why would he take off like that? And who would want to kill Sunny? Granted, Sunny was a womanizer, a lecher even, but he had a certain boyish charm.

Under all these outerwear thoughts lay the underwear thoughts. How were Maggie and Paul holding up? Didn't they have enough problems without a homicide landing in their lap? And what about Jack? Poor, vulnerable, easygoing Jack, escaping each night from godknowswhat into his sci-fi fantasy world via paperbacks. I'd always wanted to find out more about that kid, but somehow I never got around to it.

There was one bright spot in this gray load of laundry. Bobby and Becca. A pair of colorful socks spinning together in the revolving dryer. Becca had visited Bobby at the hospital. And tomorrow, she told me, she was taking him some reflectors and a headlight for his bike that she had bought with her own allowance.

Another soggy thought: I still hadn't read the riot act to Bobby's parents about their son's bad biking habits. Sigh. No use. Sleep was out of the question. I slipped out of bed and began to dress in the dark.

At first I thought I was just going for a ride. I did that sometimes when I couldn't sleep. When I'd first come to Bayfield, Sophie's death had haunted me every night—the minute my work was done and I was alone with my thoughts. I used to take long fast rides until the wind whipped the dark thoughts from my mind and my body grew so tired I'd fall into bed like a lump of cement and lose consciousness. But tonight the cause was different.

I didn't realize where I was headed until I rolled up to Harry's Bar. It was still open, but just barely. All the tables and booths were empty. There were a couple of regulars still hanging on to the bar, but the bartender was cleaning up around them.

"Seen any bikers tonight?" I asked him.

"No, thank god," he grunted.

I rode on to the Blue Arrow—the one place in Bayfield where you could get coffee and a hamburger twenty-four hours a day. The waitress told me a biker had just left. "He stocked up on sandwiches and bottled water," she said. "Seemed in a hurry."

"Which way did he go?"

She wasn't sure but thought he'd turned left. "Those hogs make such a racket, you can't help but notice them." She had probably noticed him for reasons other than the racket, but I didn't argue the point.

I took off after him, also making a left. It was five minutes before I caught sight of a single red taillight. I had barely registered the light when it disappeared. The biker had turned right—into the wilderness of shrubs and phragmites that make up most of south

Jersey. I counted slowly to twenty, not wanting to get too close, turned off my headlamp, and followed him.

Right now I didn't need my lamp. A full moon illuminated the road and every leaf and twig. But I knew once it set and dawn drew near—*It's always darkest before the dawn*—(who said that?)—a mist would rise from the marshes, like steam from a pot, and obliterate the landscape with its white blur.

In a few minutes, I sighted the red dot, and I was convinced it belonged to Pi. Although I was riding with no light, I kept my distance. I knew the moonlight would render me perfectly visible. And there was no way I could hide the noise of my motor. I hoped the noise of Pi's own motor would drown out mine. I wondered what he would do if I caught up with him. I wasn't afraid of him exactly, but I had a healthy respect for his brawn. As the dankness of the marsh crept under my jacket, I wondered briefly why I was out here. What made me think this guy was innocent? *Because he had been my paper boy?* Pretty thin. But what could have been his motive? From what I'd seen, he seemed to be fond of Sunny. I had plenty of time to think about this as I followed the red pinprick of light through the desolate marshland. The marshes weren't really desolate, of course. The foliage on either side of me was teeming with as much life as Macy's at Christmastime: birds, fish, amphibians, small mammals, and insects of every description. I had only to pause for one second to find out about the insects; hordes of mosquitoes would zero in on every part of me that wasn't covered by denim or leather. And in my haste, I'd forgotten my bug spray.

As we followed the creeks, the road twisted and turned. Now and then I lost sight of Pi's taillight. The moon was fading and darkness was closing in. I was afraid I'd have to turn on my headlamp to avoid ending up in a gully or ditch. When I'd left the Blue Arrow, I'd gotten my second wind. And in the excitement of finding my prey, my exhaustion had disappeared. But it was back again. Slumped in my seat, I felt drowsy and numb. *Snap out of it!* I sat up straight, inhaled the dank fishy smell of the marsh, and fixed my gaze on the little red dot bobbing ahead of me among the reeds.

CHAPTER 18

The darkness deepened as I had predicted, and the mist began to rise from the creeks and seep out of the marshes. At one point the fog became so dense I was forced to turn on my headlamp. The beam bounced back at me as if hitting concrete. I turned off the lamp. Sometimes the mist seemed to be stalking me, rising in front and behind, encircling, trapping me in a cotton wool cell. Then the road would open up suddenly, presenting a clear path ahead, and I'd tear along for a while thinking I had escaped, only to meet up with the fog again—as if it had taken a secret shortcut and was lying in wait for me.

Once, as I broke out of an especially dense patch, there was no taillight ahead. I traveled for a long stretch, probing the darkness, but it didn't reappear. Maybe he'd turned off somewhere and I'd lost him. To make matters worse, *I* was lost. I turned on my lamp, but there were no familiar landmarks. Nothing but low scrub and phragmites stretching to the horizon. Without that small red beacon in front of me, my desolation was complete. Until now, I hadn't realized what a comfort it was. The sign of another human being in this no-man's-land. I glanced at my gas gauge. The needle was dangerously low. I pulled over and stopped. As soon as I turned off the motor, the silence overcame me. No distant rumble of Pi's motor. There was nothing but a smothering hush. In this hour before dawn no bird chirped, no animal rustled, even the mosquitoes had left off their incessant humming. I glanced over my shoulder to see if the foul fiend was after me, ready to pounce—that black aura of failure and guilt that had forced me to leave Manhattan and come to this desolate place. Was it out there, shrouded by mist, waiting to wrap me in its damp, sour arms and drag me down into the abyss?

"Bullshit!" I grunted. "Next you'll be seeing the Jersey Devil!" Sightings of that mythical monster—half goat, half gargoyle—were often reported by the natives in these parts. I turned on the ignition. *What's the worst that can happen? You'll run out of gas and be stuck here until daylight, when someone will come along and rescue you.* The mist was dissipating already. There was a clear stretch of road ahead. I turned up the throttle and sped along. I'd just keep going until I either found a landmark or ran out of gas. Pausing at a fork in the road, I let my motor idle while I tried to decide which way to go. To my right, I thought I glimpsed part of a wharf that looked like Stow Creek Landing. Yes. And there was the creek, straight ahead. This wharf had been used by pirates and smugglers in the old days. According to legend there had been a tavern here favored by Blackbeard and his cronies. Later, bars and a bawdy house had replaced the old pirate inn and it was rumored that an occasional stabbing was not uncommon. Still later, a religious man bought the property, tore everything down but the old wharf, and planted winter wheat. Recently the state had taken over the fields, turning them into a nature preserve and picnic ground.

Despite the sanitizing of this place by the government, in the dark—just before dawn—I wouldn't have been surprised to see the ghosts of some pirates or smugglers or whores rise up and try to reclaim their turf. To keep my spirits up I let out a resounding chorus of, "Sixteen men on a dead man's chest, yo ho ho and a bottle of rum!"

A figure flew out of the phragmites. Huge hands grabbed my shoulders and shook me violently. You know that saying, "He shook me till my teeth rattled." Well, it's bunk. My teeth were just fine. It was my brain that was rattling around inside my skull, like marbles in a pinball machine.

"Sta . . . ah . . . ah . . . ahp!" I cried.

The hands let go. Pi stared at me.

I tried to catch my breath. By some miracle I was still in my bike seat.

"*Why are you following me?*" In the dark, his eyes glowed red and his astonishment was so great he forgot to swear.

I raised my hands in a protective gesture, afraid he was going to start shaking me again. "The police are looking for you!"

"What d'ya mean? I didn't do anything."

"I didn't say you did, but you have to go back and talk to them." His expression hardened.

"They'll come after you. Use your head."

"Fuck you!" Any vestige of the love-struck Archie was gone without a trace.

"Why did you take off?" I persisted.

He stared, examining my face carefully in the first light of dawn. Finally deciding to risk it, he said, "After I left the hospital, I went for a long ride. I felt like celebrating, because Sunny was OK. He was a pain in the butt, but he was sort of a kid brother to me . . ." He paused and looked away. "When I got back to the motel the place was full of cops. At first I thought they'd been called in 'cause of the party. Then I saw Sunny . . ." He winced. With a shock, I realized the extent of his grieving. "I went a little crazy and beat it."

After a moment, I said, "But you planned to stay away. You bought supplies—"

"How do you know that?" His face was hard again.

I told him about the waitress at the diner.

"Why don't you mind your own fucking business!"

"Because I want to help you!" To my horror, I realized I was screaming.

He stared. "Why?"

Forcing down a surge of emotion, which had come from who

knows where, I shrugged and said lightly, "For all those newspapers you threw at our front porch—and missed."

I was rewarded with a fleeting smile—a small shadow of Archie. He turned and dragged his bike from the phragmities where he had hidden it before he ambushed me.

"You're coming back?"

He turned. "Are you crazy?"

"But—"

"I'm outta here. I'll be in Arizona in three days. I have friends there where I can hide out."

"The police know your license number. They'll stop you before you get out of Jersey."

"I'll trash it."

"They'll pick you up for not having a tag."

"I'll think of something." He mounted his bike.

"Wait," I said desperately. "I have another idea."

"If it's anything like your others . . ."

"I know a place. There's this piece of Jersey land that actually belongs to the state of Delaware. It's a long story, but you'd be safe there. The Jersey state troopers wouldn't be able to touch you. Trust me. You could hide out there until they find out who really killed Sunny."

"Where is it?" he said slowly.

I had his attention; I rushed on. "That's the beauty of it. It's right near here. About ten miles down the road. I could supply you with food and drink and keep you up-to-date on what's going on—"

"Why would you do that?"

I wasn't sure. A mixture of loyalty to that kid from the past who used to beat me at gin rummy and a desire to see Sunny's real killer brought to justice? I said, "That's my business," and held his gaze. "Let's go. It's getting light."

And it was. The sky at the horizon was turning pink. Without waiting for an answer, I pressed my start-up button. I heard him kick-start his bike. I was afraid to look back. I just kept going, willing him to follow—and praying I could find this place. I hadn't been paying much attention when Paul had told me about it.

THURSDAY

CHAPTER 19

Murder or no murder, life must go on, even at a seedy two-star motel in south Jersey. Rugs must be vacuumed; beds must be changed; towels, toilet paper, and mini soap bars must be replenished—and wastebaskets emptied. Even a no-account motel doctor must attend to her patients. After only a few hours' sleep, I rose and went to the hospital to see Bobby. He was reading a comic book.

"Hi!" I said.

He glanced up.

"Becca's coming today."

He looked pleased.

I asked if his parents were coming.

A shadow crossed his face. "I guess," he said, without enthusiasm.

I drew nearer to get a better look at the comic book. "Who's your favorite superhero?"

He held up the magazine, cover foremost. Batman was displayed banging the heads of two ugly thugs together.

"Good choice," I said, wishing I had the skills of Batman; there were a few heads I'd like to break that morning. I glanced at my watch. Next stop—a routine nursing home call in Bridgeton.

. . .

As I rode, I tried not to think too much about Pi. When I'd left him at dawn, it was not in the most luxurious surroundings. He was sitting in a sandy clearing, hemmed in by phragmites—that tough, light-colored, ten-to-twelve-foot reed with a top like a feather duster that grows wild in south Jersey. Nearby lay a culvert, half-buried in the sand. Its entrance was a yard wide—big enough to hide Pi and his bike, if anyone should pass by, which was an unlikely prospect. A lonelier spot was hard to imagine.

When I'd left him, he was eating his breakfast—a stale ham on rye washed down with warm beer. (He had managed to stash a six-pack in his saddlebag, along with the sandwiches and bottled water.) He was especially unhappy with the temperature of the brew. I pointed out that he was only a few yards from the bay, where he could cool it if he wanted to.

He grunted.

I told him I'd return with fresh supplies after dark. As I pulled away, I glanced back once. Sitting cross-legged in the sand, with his barrel chest and thick thighs, surrounded by phragmites, he looked like a Buddha some archaeologist had dug up and abandoned when he found it was too heavy to carry.

Although it was just a routine call, I always looked forward to seeing Emily Snow. (Her cloud of white hair made her last name especially fitting.) She had taught American history at the local high school for over thirty years and local history was her hobby. Nothing had happened in Bayfield that Emily didn't know and wasn't willing to tell you about since the Lenape Indians had settled there. It was from Emily I heard about the pirates and smugglers who had frequented these parts. She had also given me a lesson on phragmites. Now considered a mere nuisance weed that drove all other vegetation away, this reed had once been put to many uses by the Lenapes. They had weaved mats with it and made shafts for their arrows, just to name a couple.

Today I had a specific question for Miss Snow. After I had examined her (which didn't take long; she was amazingly healthy for her age), I asked it.

She laughed. "So, you've discovered our secret. Our double identity." She stared out the window for a moment before going on. "Yes—part of Bayfield still belongs to Delaware, and no one has ever felt it was important enough to change. Except during the Oyster Wars, of course," she added.

"Oyster Wars?"

"Yes, indeed. Oysters were a big industry here in the nineties [I knew she meant the 1890s] and the two states fought over the beds. We finally got access to some of the best beds, but it was a hard fight. It took years."

I pulled out my county map and spread it across her knees.

"Oh, yes." She peered at the map, using the little magnifying glass she always kept on a string around her neck. "See here." She pointed to a bit of land that poked into the bay. "That belongs to Delaware, but it's next to the nuclear power plant. I'm sure no one can get near there today. Security must be wicked." She moved her finger northward to a large green sward bordering the bay. "Now, this is mostly wilderness. Marshes and tidelands—and mosquitoes!" She laughed, glancing up at me. "If you're thinking of exploring there, be sure to take along plenty of bug spray."

I began to refold the map.

"So why this sudden interest in our geography, Doctor?" She fixed her penetrating gaze on me.

I shrugged. "I've always liked history and geography—"

"Liar."

I blinked.

"I've taught enough children over the years to know when one's fibbing."

I was about to protest that I wasn't a child when I realized, to someone nearly ninety I probably was.

"Besides," she went on, "I remember you once sat right in that chair and told me you hated history and geography in school."

"But that was because I had lousy teachers. Now . . . if I'd had *you!*"

"Flattery will get you nowhere." She tapped her front tooth with her magnifying glass and eyed me suspiciously.

I sighed. "I'm sure glad you weren't *my* teacher."

She shot me a quick grin. "Years ago, that area I just showed you was used for all kinds of illicit activities—bootlegging, prostitution. Now it's probably a haven for drug peddlers—and growers," she said.

I *thought* I'd seen a marijuana field on the way there.

"New Jersey law enforcers can't touch them—unless they extradite them. And that would be much too much trouble. The Feds could, of course, but they've got their hands full in Philadelphia." She laughed. This lady not only knew her history; she also was up on current events. "Someday when land gets really scarce and that area becomes valuable to developers, it will be a different story."

I was tempted to confide in her. I was fond of the old lady. I respected and trusted her. I was sure my secret would be safe with her.

"There was a murder at the Oakview Motor Lodge," I said tentatively.

"Yes, I know." She subscribed to both the Salem and Bridgeton papers as well as *The Philadelphia Inquirer.* She didn't miss much. But unlike Mrs. Lockweed, she wasn't a gossip. She kept things to herself.

"They suspect one of the bikers who are staying there," I said.

She looked at me speculatively. "And you don't think he did it."

I stared. She *was* sharp. I nodded.

Even though there were just the two of us in the room, she lowered her voice, "And you're looking for a place to hide him."

My mouth dropped open. "How did you know?"

"Because," she said firmly, "that's what I would do."

"He's already in that safe Delaware area, but he can't stay there forever with no roof over his head. I wondered if you knew of any shelter . . ."

She was thoughtful. "Let me see that map again."

I spread it out. She studied it in silence. "There used to be a fisherman's shack right about here." She pointed. "It's been abandoned for years. But if it hasn't fallen down by now, it might just do." She took a pencil from beside her chair where she had been working a crossword puzzle and began tracing the route I should take.

When she finished, she looked so pleased with herself, I had to ask, "How do you know about this?"

She smiled. "It belonged to a man I once knew. We," she hastily corrected herself, "*he* used to camp out there in the old days."

I couldn't stop my grin.

"Oh—you young people think you invented romance," she said, and waved a deprecating hand. Then she turned serious. "But you'd better not waste any time. All the police need is a governor's warrant to extradite a fugitive from another state." I headed for the door and she went back to her crossword puzzle.

"Wait," she called me back. "You're a doctor. What's a five-letter word for 'a device that keeps arteries open'?"

"*Stent.*"

"Perfect. Thanks."

"Don't mention it."

CHAPTER 20

While in Bridgeton, I decided to look up Jack and ask him if he'd noticed anything unusual the night Sunny was killed. I knew the night clerk rented an apartment on Pearl Street in a building that was even seedier than the Oakview Motor Lodge. Until now, I had only seen it from the outside. The frame house was loaded with gingerbread and would have been a fine example of Victorian architecture except for its sagging porch and peeling paint.

I hit the button next to Jack's name. After a minute a sleepy, disembodied voice jarred me. "Yeah?"

"Oh, hi, Jack. It's Jo. I'm sorry. I forgot you work nights and sleep late. Stupid of me." I glanced at my watch. Only 9:30.

"No prob. I'll buzz you in."

Jack's apartment surprised me. Neat and cheerful, the walls were covered with bright posters of *Star Wars* and other sci-fi films. He had a TV, a VCR, and a DVD player. A bookcase housed multiple videos and DVDs. He was obviously updating his film collection. He wore jeans and a tee, but his feet were bare. He had probably thrown on his clothes quickly while I was coming up the stairs. He pulled out a chair for me. "Want some coffee? All I have is instant," he apologized.

"No, thanks. I'm sorry I woke you. I wanted to talk to you about last night."

He slumped onto his futon. "I wasn't much help," he muttered.

"Neither was I," I said.

He was quiet, eyes cast down.

"Did you hear, they think Sunny was poisoned?"

He looked up.

"And Pi is under suspicion because he skipped out."

"Holy shit!"

"Exactly." I let that sink in before I went on. "What I want to know is if you saw anything suspicious last night. Like somebody fooling with Sunny's drinks . . ."

He brushed a strand of hair from his eyes. "God, everything was so crazy. I was afraid those guys were going to tear the place apart."

"Me, too."

He closed his eyes, thinking. After a moment he said, "I was sitting at the desk. Most of the action was outside. I could hear it—and see some of it through the glass door. Now and then one of them would burst in to grab a beer or pee. They were drinking stronger stuff, too. I saw at least one bottle of bourbon."

I nodded.

"And there was plenty of pot floating around."

Again I nodded.

"Finally I couldn't stand it anymore and I went outside to see what was happening."

"I saw you."

He looked sheepish. "And I came right back inside."

"Smartest thing you could've done."

"And called nine-one-one."

"Good for you. I tried to, but I dropped my cell when Sunny grabbed me."

"That was pretty cool, what Canby did." He grinned. "Oh, I'm sure it wasn't cool for you. I mean, what if he'd missed?"

"Yeah, but he didn't." I returned his grin. "Can you remember who came into the lobby?"

"I don't know many of those guys. Only Pi, and Sunny and a couple of others. They all look pretty much alike."

"Ugly."

"Yeah."

I glanced around the room. "You have a nice place here. I don't suppose you have any interest in science fiction?"

He blushed. "You might call it an obsession."

I picked up a worn paperback from the table and looked at the title. *Classic Science Fiction Stories.* "I've never read much sci-fi. Could I borrow this?"

"Help yourself. I . . ." He paused.

"What?"

"We science fiction buffs don't like the term *sci-fi,*" he said, half apologetically. "It's usually used by people who make fun of us."

"Oh? Sorry. I didn't know."

"That's OK." He hesitated, then said in a rush, "Iwritestories."

"No kidding."

"I have a drawer full of rejection slips."

"That's fabulous!" So, I was wrong again. Just like with Becca. She hadn't been running off to New York to get away from Bay-field. She'd been going to Manhattan to study the skyscrapers, in the hope of becoming an architect. And Jack wasn't escaping into sci-fi fiction; he was honing his craft by reading good sci-fi writers. I thought everyone was running away because I was. "Someone told me once that if you don't get rejection slips on a regular basis, you're not a professional writer."

"Then I'm a *real* professional." Jack smiled.

"Could I read one?"

"What?"

"One of your stories."

"Oh—" He was suddenly shy. "I dunno. . . ."

"I'd really like to."

He got up and went over to a battered filing cabinet in a corner of the room. He came back with a manuscript. I read the title. "The Little Green Man." I was already hooked. "Thanks. I'll take good care of it."

He shrugged. Like any professional writer, he probably had several copies, on either paper or disk. "I'd better be going. If you think of anything else you saw last night, let me know."

As he let me out, he said, "That guest—the only guy there that's not a biker?—was hanging around the lobby for a while."

"Stan?"

"Yeah. He kept peeking out the door. I don't think he'd ever seen anything like it."

"Who had?" I laughed.

He joined me. "But after awhile he really got into the swing of it. Was opening bottles and handing them to the guys. . . ."

As I walked to my bike I thought how little I'd learned about Sunny's murder and how much I'd learned about Jack.

CHAPTER 21

When I walked in to pick up my mail, the motel was abuzz. Paul Nelson was in his office talking earnestly to Detective Peck. Maggie was counting sheets, while Theresa and Marie, the two maids, were setting off in opposite directions with piles of clean towels. A bunch of bikers, Jingles among them, were horsing around the soda machine. No one paid any attention to me until I turned to leave.

"Dr. Banks?"

I turned back and saw Peck coming toward me. When he reached me, he lowered his voice. "Have you heard anything from our illustrious Apostle leader?"

I shook my head.

He gave me a keen look. For a boondocks detective, he was no bumpkin. I had read a book once by a guy who had made a life study of facial expressions. Interviewed tribes in the back ends of Africa, Australia, and South America and discovered certain similarities among members of the human race. One was, we blink more often when we're lying. I tried to keep from blinking while Peck stared at me. Another thing this scholar had studied was body language. According to him, liars often make furtive involuntary movements with their hands and feet. I stood rigidly still.

"A word of warning, Doctor. Withholding evidence and aiding a suspect are serious offenses with grave consequences."

He was good. Almost as good as Emily Snow. I felt the sweat trickle down my back. As Peck turned away, someone called my name from across the room.

Jingles.

I waited, watching him slide toward me. His stringy red beard looked stringier than usual and there were pouches under his eyes. "We have a problem." He leaned in real close, giving me the full benefit of his body odor. "They're releasing Sunny's body tomorrow and we're planning a little send-off for him. Do you know a patch of ground with, say, a shade tree and maybe a few daisies?"

I examined Jingles's face carefully, the way the detective had examined mine. Not for signs of deceit, but for any signs of human feeling. I found none. "I'll look into it," I said.

"We're pickin' Sunny up at eight A.M. We need to know before that. My room number's seventeen."

His color wasn't good and his face showed strain. Maybe he had suffered some loss. Who was I to judge? "I'll see what I can do."

He left without a word of thanks.

I shrugged and headed for Maggie. She had stopped counting sheets and was staring into space—in another world. As I drew near, I saw a tear glisten on her cheek. She wiped it quickly away when I came up.

"Mag?"

She focused on me.

"Anything wrong?"

She smiled, a wry smile.

"I know. Everything."

"Detective Peck has been grilling us all morning. Nick's case went to the jury today. And Paul . . ." She swallowed hard.

I wanted to hug her, but with all the people milling around the lobby, I hesitated. Instead, I patted her hand. Paul was sitting a few yards away, studiously reading the paper. "Is Paul going with you tomorrow?" I asked loudly.

She shook her head.

"Well," I said cheerfully, "since you don't have any problems, I have one for you." If I could distract her from her own troubles for even a few minutes, it might help. "I need a grave site."

She looked startled.

I told her about Jingles's request. It worked. She wrinkled her brow, giving the problem her full attention. "I don't know any farmer who would give up part of his precious field," she said slowly, "but I do know a patch of woods . . ." She laid the pile of sheets aside and went into the office. I watched her pick up the phone and dial. (They still had a rotary phone.) While she talked, Paul continued to read his paper. When she came back she looked pleased. "I found something. Ed Potter has a clearing in a patch of woods behind his house. He and his boys—"

"Ah, the Potter boys. They're the ones who found the first scarecrow."

"That's right." A cloud crossed her face as she was reminded of the crimes her son was accused of. One of which was doping immigrant workers and hanging them in fields disguised as scarecrows—until they died of exposure.

I bit my tongue. "Is Mr. Potter willing?" I asked hastily.

She nodded. "He's a reverent man. He said, 'Even outlaws, like those bikers, deserve a decent burial.' "

"That's very kind—"

"Now, what about a preacher? I can ask mine. Reverend Dunbar. Do you know what kind of service—?"

"I'll check," I interrupted. "But I don't think a preacher will be necessary. Bikers have their own traditions."

"You mean like the Quakers?"

Pi's description of Crazy Freddy's funeral came back to me and I remembered that the Quakers specialized in silent meditation. "Not exactly," I said. "Thanks, Mag. You've been a big help." I took off in search of Jingles.

I found him in the parking lot, mounting his bike. I gave him Maggie's information and told him where the patch of woods was located. "I know your funerals are pretty wild," I said. "I hope you'll try to keep this one low-key."

"Sure, Doc." His smile bordered on a sneer. "I'll see that it's real dignified." He revved his motor. "Think I'll take a look-see at that grave site right now. Make sure it's up to par."

A sudden thought came to me. "Does Sunny have any family?"

An odd look crossed his face. "None that would claim him."

"But shouldn't they be notified?"

"I took care of that." He disappeared in a cloud of exhaust.

Jingles seemed to be in charge now, taking over Pi's place. I wondered how the other bikers liked that.

CHAPTER 22

I checked my watch. Only 11:30. Plenty of time before office hours to poke around and ask a few questions. I decided to tackle Marie. Motel staff often heard and saw things that other people missed, primarily because the guests often treated them as if they were furniture. While I was searching for her, my cell phone rang. Tom's lawyer friend wanted to meet with us in his office at 4:30. Since my office hours weren't over until 4:00, this would be cutting it close. I told him I might be a few minutes late.

"Hi, Doc." Marie rattled by trundling her supply cart at breakneck speed.

"Hey, wait!" I caught up with her. "Do you have a minute?"

"Sure." Marie was always happy to stop working.

I looked up and down the hall and lowered my voice. "I'm trying to find out if anyone saw anything suspicious the day Sunny died."

"You working on that biker's murder?"

Marie knew I'd helped break the immigrant scam. "Sort of. Unofficially."

"Be careful, Doc. Those bikers are tough."

I nodded impatiently

"I did hear one funny thing today," she said. "That guy with the red beard—"

"Jingles."

"Was talking to the bruiser with the tattoos—"

"They all have tattoos."

"This one has more!"

"Hammerhead."

"I was running the vacuum, and when I stopped I overheard Red Beard say something about a poison pie."

"What?"

"Yeah. He said, 'I think pie poisoned him.' Do you think he got a bad slice at the diner?" She looked quizzical.

Not pie but Pi? I translated. "Maybe," I said. "Anything else?"

"No. As soon as they noticed the vacuum was off, they shut up and beat it."

"Thanks, Marie. Any luck getting in there?" I nodded at the door of the odd couple's room next to mine.

She shook her head in disgust.

"Don't they ever come out?"

"I think they do, but they're too lazy to take the Do Not Disturb sign off the door."

"Have you tried knocking?"

Her eyes widened. "Once I did, and they were inside. The wife cursed me out something terrible!"

I smiled. "Better let it go. Besides, what do you care if they want to live like pigs?"

"Because when they leave, *I* have to clean their pigsty," she said sulkily.

I patted her arm.

So Jingles was spreading the rumor that Pi had done Sunny in. *Bastard.* I let myself into my room. A glance in the mirror told me I looked just as bad as I felt—as if I hadn't eaten or slept for two days! I wonder why. I kicked off my shoes and, at the risk of wrinkling my one professional pantsuit, stretched out full-length on the futon and closed my eyes. Who should I talk to next?

The bikers. My lids snapped open. *Of course. Why am I so dense?* I didn't believe that any of them had done Sunny in, but they might have seen or heard something useful. I dragged myself off the futon, shoved my feet back in my shoes, and set out again.

As I opened my door, Honey and Hammerhead sauntered by, talking earnestly.

"Have a minute?" I stopped them.

"Sure, Doc. What's up?" Honey stepped back a few paces.

"Do either of you know anyone who might have had it in for Sunny?"

Hammerhead rolled his eyes.

"No disrespect to the dead," Honey reproved him.

"Seriously."

They exchanged glances. Were they remembering the scene when Pi threw Sunny unceremoniously out of the lobby? But neither spoke. First one, then the other, shrugged.

"Just thought I'd ask." I watched them continue down the hall, with their bowlegged gait. All those hours spent on a bike were like riding horseback, I guess. That's why they called them ponies. Duh.

I went in search of more bikers. I had a feeling of urgency now. I'd heard nothing more about Peck's "other leads" and I wasn't sure how much longer Pi would be willing to put up with his modest living quarters.

CHAPTER 23

My first patient was a surprise. Detective Peck stood up as I entered the waiting room.

"Not sick, I hope," I said.

"Not at the moment. I'm here on another matter."

"Come on in." I gestured for him to follow me into my consulting room—an area two square feet smaller than the waiting room, which was the size of a closet. I sat down behind my desk and waited uneasily for him to say what was on his mind.

"You've been doing some sleuthing, I understand."

I tried to maintain a poker face, but my facial muscles were worn out from a morning's lying. "A little," I admitted, "if you call asking a few questions, 'sleuthing.' "

"I don't want you meddling." His expression was stern. "Just because you got lucky with that immigrant case doesn't make you Sherlock Holmes."

I would hardly call myself "lucky" to have been tortured and almost killed, but I kept silent. "But I might be able to learn things you can't," I said reasonably, "since I'm living on the premises."

"What things?"

"Who was where, when, what they said, did . . . I don't know. . . ." I shrugged. "I'm a pretty good eavesdropper."

He grunted. "Eavesdropping is one thing; directly interrogating people is another." He studied his shoes thoughtfully. When he looked up, he said, "What have you heard so far?"

"Red Beard, alias Jingles, is stirring things up, casting suspicion on people—"

"What people?"

"Oh, various bikers . . ." I wasn't about to bring Pi into the picture.

"Are you going to the funeral?" Peck asked.

I blinked. Actually, I hadn't thought about it until now. "I wasn't planning on . . ."

"Why don't you?" he said abruptly. "Your eavesdropping techniques might prove useful—and you won't stand out the way I or a trooper would."

"Having a change of heart, Mr. Peck?"

"As long as you share your findings with me . . . *all* your findings . . . I don't see any harm in your going."

The bell on the front door tinkled. A real patient.

"I won't keep you any longer." Peck rose. "Just remember, everything you learn is shared with me immediately." He handed me a card bearing his office, home and cell numbers. "Call me anytime. Day or night."

It took me a few minutes to recover from the detéctive's impromptu visit. I had to ask Mrs. Lockweed to repeat her symptoms twice, much to her annoyance.

"You feeling all right, Doctor?" Mrs. Lockweed was staring at me.

"Just a little tired," I muttered. "Let me give you that prescription." I pulled out a prescription blank and—following a long, time-honored tradition—wrote down the information in an unreadable scrawl.

As I rushed through the lobby, heading for the appointment with Wosky, I noticed the front desk was empty. Odd. Paul or Maggie always took the afternoon shift. There was usually some cash in the desk drawer. While I was debating what to do, a sound came from the laundry room. Something between a moan and a sob. I went over and pulled open the door. Maggie looked up, her face puffy and wet.

"Mag!" I started to put my arm around her, but she pushed me away.

"I can't take any more, Jo," she said. "I just can't. First the trial—and now this!" She broke into loud, gasping sobs.

I shut the door behind me. It wouldn't do to have the whole staff thinking their boss was cracking up. "What happened?"

She took a deep breath. "That man was in here again, questioning everyone—"

"Peck?"

She nodded. "He thinks that biker was poisoned. He made me show him all the closets. And he found some rat poison. We always keep some with the cleaning supplies. Not for rats, mind you—only mice!"

I wasn't sure which Maggie resented more—the invasion of her privacy or the insult to her housekeeping. "Is that the only thing that's worrying you?"

She didn't answer right away. Then she said quietly, "The jury is out. A verdict is expected tomorrow."

I moved some towels and sat down next to her. "Is Paul going with you?"

She shook her head.

"Damn him!" For once Maggie didn't frown at my expletive. "I'll come with you," I said.

She looked up. "Would you?"

"Of course. But I think Paul should go. I can't believe that man. What's wrong with him?"

She looked away.

I glanced at my watch. "Lord—I have to run. Don't worry; whatever happens, I guarantee you won't be alone tomorrow."

As I left, I wished I would bump into Paul so I could give him a piece of my mind. I loved the old man. And I sympathized with his feelings about his no-good son. But enough was enough. Paul's place tomorrow was with his wife.

But Paul was nowhere in sight and I was going to be late for that appointment. Mounting my bike, I pressed the start-up button and turned the throttle up to the max.

CHAPTER 24

The session with the lawyer was brief. After listening to the account of my visit from Peck, Wosky was convinced neither Tom nor I was regarded seriously as a suspect.

"Keep clear of the bikers and go about your business. And under no circumstances attend that funeral," was Wosky's sage advice. That's what you pay lawyers for—advice, right? It doesn't mean you have to follow it.

As we left the office, Tom said, "Dinner?"

"Better not," I stalled. "Have to pick up some groceries."

"Want company?"

Oh, hell. If he came along how could I buy a six-pack and a carton of Marlboros without making him suspicious? I'd have to fake it and make two shopping trips. Oh, well, deception was becoming second nature. "Sure," I said.

As we cruised the aisles and I picked out stuff I didn't need: soap, cereal, ketchup, Tom told me about a surprise he was working on for me.

I paused between the soup and canned vegetables. "What is it?"

"If I tell you, it won't be a surprise, dope."

"Phooey."

Glancing swiftly up and down the aisle, he grabbed and kissed me. I leaned into him and thought how nice it would be to forget about Pi, have a leisurely dinner, and go home with Tom.

"Excuse me!" a cranky woman's voice interrupted us. We broke apart with sheepish looks. The woman pushed her cart past us with a disapproving stare. We stifled our giggles.

In the dairy section, Tom dropped a carton of low-fat yogurt into my cart.

"Hey, what makes you think I need that?"

"It's good for you."

"Are you implying I'm fat?"

He stepped back to better survey me. "Hmm." He scratched his head.

I was about to ram him with my cart but thought better of it. No point attracting attention. Especially when I planned to return here shortly for another load. Instead I yawned and glanced at my watch. "I've gotta get back. Bed is calling."

"Change your mind about dinner?"

I shook my head.

Disappointed, he followed me through the checkout. "Since when do you need so much sleep? I thought doctors were used to surviving on two or three hours."

"Young interns," I said. "But middle-aged practitioners like me need their full eight hours."

Resigned, he didn't press me anymore, and we parted in the parking lot. I packed the first load of groceries in my saddlebag before returning to the market. This time I made a point of going to a different checker. It was quite a feat to pack two loads of groceries in one saddlebag. As I nosed my top-heavy bike into the road, I cursed Tom *and* Pi.

Despite my unwieldy burden, I stopped at the hospital to check on Bobby. Becca was still there. She had brought her Game Boy and the two kids were happily absorbed in a game. Bobby's dinner sat untouched on a tray nearby. When I came in they both looked up and smiled.

"I'm getting out tomorrow," Bobby said.

"Shouldn't you eat your dinner before it gets cold?" My irritable tone surprised even me.

Bobby's smile vanished. "Oh, yeah." He pulled the tray toward him and began unwrapping a plastic fork.

I turned on Becca. "And don't you have homework to do?"

She frowned and muttered, "What's your problem?"

"What was that?"

"Nothing." She began packing up her knapsack.

A sullen silence enveloped the room. Shit. What *was* my problem? Unable or unwilling to analyze it, I asked Bobby a few cursory questions about his health and left, having successfully ruined two people's evening.

As I lugged my unneeded groceries up to the second floor, Paul had the misfortune to cross my path.

"Hi, Jo," he said. "Can I help you with those?"

I shook my head and planted myself in his way.

"What's up?" he asked warily.

"Why aren't you going to court with Maggie tomorrow?"

He stared. "I never go to court."

"Are you proud of that?"

"What d'ya mean?"

"Your wife is suffering the tortures of the damned and you behave like a goddamned ostrich."

He was silent.

"Your son is going to be sentenced tomorrow—"

He glared and spit out the words, *"I . . . don't . . . have . . . a . . . son."*

"Oh, *excuse* me. I was misinformed." I pushed past him.

"Why don't you mind your own business!" he shouted after me.

I kept going.

CHAPTER 25

By the time I had stored my groceries and repacked Pi's it was getting dark. Almost dark enough to set off on my errand of mercy. I had forgotten to buy bug spray, so I took my own half-empty can. No sacrifice was too great! I avoided the lobby because I knew Jack was on duty. I didn't want him asking where I was going and have to lie again. Lying was becoming too easy. Besides, I hadn't read his story yet, and I knew he'd be disappointed.

I trundled my bike onto the main road. It was lighter without the extra load of groceries, but not much, because I had added a cooler full of ice so Pi could have his beer chilled.

I had called him on my cell phone before leaving, and he had sounded despondent. I was worried how much longer he would be willing to put up with the poor accommodations. When I told him about the cabin, he perked up. "Does it have a fridge?" he asked.

"Don't expect miracles," I said, and his glum mood returned. That's when I decided to bring the cooler of ice.

The ride to the hideout was almost uneventful. I took a circuitous route to foil any followers. Once I thought a pickup was tailing me, but when I looked again it had disappeared. My overloaded saddlebag slowed me down. I was looking forward to the ride home, when my bike would be denuded and light again.

"Yo!" I yelled into the darkness at a spot approximately where I thought I had left Pi. There was no answer. Pulling out my flashlight, I sprayed the area with light.

"Shut that fucking thing off!" A dark figure emerged from one end of the culvert and stepped into my pool of light. "Do you want all the skeeters in Jersey coming here for dinner?"

I tossed him the can of bug spray. He lunged at it like a drowning man and began squirting himself all over. The sight of a tough biker panicking because of a few bugs might have been humorous under different circumstances, but I wasn't in a humorous mood. I took out the map on which Miss Snow had outlined the route to the cabin and said, "When you're done, let's go."

He tossed the can at me and dragged his bike from inside the culvert. I revved up and took the lead. We putted single file over rough sandy roads walled in by tall banks of phragmites. Once, afraid we might be lost, I stopped to check Miss Snow's map with my flashlight. After what seemed like hours but was only about twenty minutes, the silhouette of a chimney rose against the lighter sky. I pulled over. Pi did the same. My flashlight beam revealed a shabby wooden shack with a screened-in porch. The screen was full of holes.

"Home Sweet Home," Pi muttered.

"At least it has a roof," I said.

"We won't know that till it rains," he grumbled.

We unloaded the supplies and began carrying the stuff inside. There was no problem getting in; the lock had rusted away long ago. There was the sound of scurrying feet, the glitter of tiny eyes, and something furry fluttered past my nose. "Yikes!" I squealed.

"Bats," Pi said. Unlike mosquitoes, bats didn't bother him.

An odor of damp and mold filled our nostrils. Pi began fighting with the windows, while I brought in the remaining supplies.

In a few minutes we had dug up a couple of ragged wicker chairs and were lounging in them, sipping *cold* beer.

"This is the life," Pi said, with heavy sarcasm.

"Count your blessings," I snapped.

"How's your snooping going?" he asked.

I was ready for that. I had made up my mind on the way out that I needed more help from him. "I need to know more about your biker brothers."

Silence.

"Look. I know all about your Code. But this is a matter of life and death."

"Death?"

"Well . . . sure." I faltered. "Sunny died, didn't he?"

No answer.

"If you don't trust me, Pi, I can't help you."

Out of habit, he squashed his beer can and reached for another. I wanted to tell him to go easy, to ration them, but decided to keep my mouth shut. I waited while he lit a Marlboro and tossed the match.

"Watch those matches," I cautioned. "This place could go up like a tinderbox."

"In this damp?"

I shut up.

"What d'ya wanna know?"

"What's your relationship to Jingles?"

He snorted.

"Seriously."

The glowing tip of his cigarette moved from his mouth to his lap several times before he spoke.

"Ever since I became president, Jingles has been a pain in the butt. A thorn in my side. Sunny was a nuisance with his fucking sex problem. But Jingles was a real bugger."

"Do you think he wants your job?"

He shrugged.

"Well, he's sure taking over now. Bossing everybody around, making snide remarks about you, arranging the funeral—"

"Funeral?"

Me and my big mouth. Reluctantly I outlined the plan for Sunny's funeral.

"What time does it start?"

"You're not thinking of going?"

"Sure. He was my brother." There was a catch in his throat.

"Pi . . ."

He took a deep swallow of beer and brushed some ash from his thigh. His silence left no doubt in my mind about his intentions.

"Do you think Jingles could have killed Sunny?" I asked.

My eyes had gotten used to the dark and I saw his eyes widen under his sleepy lids. I was reminded of the raw intelligence behind them. "No way."

"What makes you so sure?"

"What's his motive? If he wants to be king he should kill me, not Sunny."

I shook my head. "Not necessarily. He just has to put you out of commission."

"By pinning the murder on me?" This was a new idea, but he caught on fast. "And with my background, he has a head start."

It was a minute before I took this in.

"I have a prison record."

Although I knew this, it occurred to me that I had never found out why Pi had served time. And here I was, alone in a cabin in the middle of nowhere with an ex-con. "What for?" I asked weakly.

Reading my mind, he laughed. "Relax, I ain't no serial killer. I sold drugs."

"At MIT?"

He nodded. "Stupid, right?"

I didn't answer at once. Then I said, "We all do stupid things." I thought of my own stupidity. Misdiagnosing a child's illness. At least Pi's stupidity hadn't killed anyone (that I knew of). "I know all about stupid things," I said, and told him about Sophie.

Unlike Tom, he was sympathetic. Told me it wasn't my fault. To forget it. But Tom was right. You do stupid things, you pay for them, he had told me. And you don't get over them. You live with them for the rest of your life.

"So what's the next move?" Pi crushed his cigarette.

"All I can do is keep my eyes open, eavesdrop, ask questions. But the detective has ok'd my going to the funeral—and says he'll keep the law away. I still don't think you should come, though, Pi. It's too risky. What if one of the bikers squeals?"

He shook his head vehemently. "They're all righteous brothers. They won't snitch. That's the worst sin a biker can do. We'd strip him of his colors, beat the shit out of him, and throw him out of the club. He'd never risk that."

I was unconvinced. But I kept my thoughts to myself.

"Don't worry. I'll stay on the sidelines. You probably won't even see me. But I gotta go. Sunny was my brother."

I drained my beer and stood. "See you—or rather . . . I *won't* see you—tomorrow."

"What time?"

"Two-thirty."

We walked out to the porch. I was surprised how light it was. The moon had risen and turned the feathery heads of the phragmites to silver. Rows of silver feather dusters dancing in the moonlight.

Pi planted a sloppy, wet kiss on my mouth—taking me by surprise. "Thanks for the stuff," he said.

"Anytime, "I said, and resisted the urge to wipe my mouth. "Banks Express Delivery at your service." I pulled on my helmet and crunched across the dirt-encrusted porch, scattering dry leaves and twigs in my wake. At the door, I turned. "Tomorrow you can pass the time by cleaning this place."

"Up yours," he said.

As I had predicted, the ride home was a breeze. Without my heavy load, the bike fairly floated. My earlier bad mood evaporated in the cool night air. I wished I could apologize to Bobby and Becca. I would make it up to them. But not Paul. My conscience was clear there. He got what he deserved. My thoughts returned to Pi and that kiss—a simple brotherly gesture of gratitude. Absolutely no sexual connotations. Tom was wrong. Men and women could be just friends. Remembering my first impression of Pi—a hairy monster with too many tattoos and body odor—I wondered at my lack of repulsion. True, I had wanted to wipe the kiss away, but not because it repulsed me. It was just too juicy. I realized I felt a strong affection for him—but no attraction. I read once that the French have many words to describe the variety of feelings men and women have for one another. We have only one. *Love.* You either love him or you don't. You either love her or you don't. Cut-and-dried. Black-and-white. Inaccurate. *Boring!*

Twisting the throttle a notch higher, I burst into song. An old Springsteen number—"Born to Run." I hope I caused some of those country folk, sleeping peacefully in their snug farmhouses, to roll over and grumble.

CHAPTER 26

As I parked in the motel lot, I heard tires crunch on gravel. A biker returning from a late-night run? A door slammed. *Bikes don't have doors.* I turned and saw Tom coming toward me.

"Hi! What . . ."

He grabbed my shoulder and looked into my face. For a split second we were frozen, as if in a camera frame. A strange, inarticulate sound came from his throat. He swiveled around and strode back to his truck.

As he drove off, the air around me pulsated with his unspent emotion.

I didn't move. I waited, letting my thoughts slowly come into focus. He must have followed me. That truck behind me, it must have been his! I thought I'd lost him, because he'd turned off his headlights and the sound of his motor had been drowned out by my own. And on the way back—I had been singing.

If he followed me, he must have seen Pi and me on the porch. My thoughts came fast, tumbling over one another. We must have been clearly visible in the moonlight. That kiss! And Tom had drawn his own conclusions. The wrong conclusions. I had to explain. I started to remount my bike and stopped. Who the hell did he think he was anyway, sneaking after me—spying on me? I gave my bike a savage kick and limped up to my room.

Violence. As I lay in bed, I thought about it. I'd never been a victim of violence. Until the bikers arrived and Sunny snatched me up and was carrying me off. My dad had never even spanked me. My worst punishment had been being sent to my room; and he never made me stay long. He missed me too much. He was a widower—and lonely.

I never had violent boyfriends. On the contrary, I was usually the one who hit them. Suddenly, within a week, I'd been assaulted with intent to rape and shaken until my brain rattled. But the thing that had upset me the most was the encounter with Tom, which had *not* erupted in violence. I shivered, feeling his suppressed emotion all over again.

I slept fitfully and woke often. Every time I woke, the room seemed alive with my agitated thoughts. I felt, if I opened my eyes, I would be able to see them, reach out, and touch them, like those bats in the fisherman's shack.

In the forefront was Tom. Half of me wanted to call him and explain about Pi. Tell him that kiss had been a mere brotherly expression of gratitude. Pi would have bussed anyone who had brought him cold beer, male or female. Sex had nothing to do with it. I could hear Tom's derisive laughter. Damn him. The other half of me wanted to murder Tom—for chasing after me, for spying on me.

Anxious thoughts about Sunny's murder followed. Time was flying. The police seemed no nearer a solution. And *I* sure wasn't getting anywhere. Pi couldn't hide out much longer. Either he would get fed up and take off, or Peck would find him and decide to begin extradition proceedings.

I thought of Emily Snow. What would she do? I could go ask her tomorrow. But she was old. Her advice might be tempered by age—failing sight, hearing loss, thinning bones, and memory lapses. Nah. She was still sharp—just like Dad.

Dad! Ohmygod! He'd called a couple of days ago—the same day Tom did—and I'd never called him back. So much had been going on. I glanced at the luminous dial of the alarm clock. Three-oh-five AM. I couldn't call him now. He'd have a heart attack. What a rat I was. Damn. Damn. Damn. My guilt filled the room like the smell of boiled cabbage.

I flicked on the light and looked frantically around for some distraction. Jack's manuscript lay on my bedside table. I snatched it up. If it was good, it would take my mind off my troubles. If it was bad, it would put me to sleep. I began to read:

The Little Green Man
By Jack Olsen

The little green man comes in many guises. He can come like a worm in an apple or like a fire in a furnace. He can nibble at your insides over a period of months and years or burst on you, scorching you in an instant…

This is pretty good, I thought. But the day's strain had finally taken its toll. My eyelids began to droop. I let the manuscript slide to the floor.

FRIDAY

CHAPTER 27

When I woke, I was surprised to find my bedside lamp still on. I flicked it off and all the events of the night before swept over me like a string of wet laundry. I pulled the sheets over my head, unready to face the day. What would it have in store for me? More wet laundry? *Slap, slap, slap*—it hit me in the face. Bobby's release, Nick's sentencing, Sunny's funeral. I felt inadequate to deal with any one of them, let alone three. I crawled out of bed and made my way to the bathroom. I postponed thinking about Tom. I couldn't handle him yet. I'd read that the way Bill Clinton survived the Lewinsky scandal was to compartmentalize. When he was dealing with the secretary of defense he thought only about defense, when dealing with his press secretary he thought only about the press, etcetera. I decided that was the only way I could get through this day. One compartment at a time.

The first challenge was to wake up. A cold shower helped (but not much). Coffee sludge got my brain working (sort of). A quick jog around the parking lot got my blood going (barely). By eight o'clock I was functioning as well as could be expected and ready for my first encounter with another human being. It came in the form of two human beings. Maggie and Paul. It was the first time I'd seen them going anywhere together for months. They were walking single file, Paul in the lead, across the parking lot toward their pickup. I trotted over and gave Maggie an encouraging hug. I watched her climb into the truck and noticed she wasn't as agile as usual. As a physician, I knew that life's crises can take their toll on the body as well as the emotions. I felt guilty for not going with her today. I had the distinct feeling Paul would not be much help. As they drove off, I waved. Maggie waved back, but Paul ignored me. *He'd get over it*, I told myself.

Encounter number two came in the lobby. Jingles. He was in high spirits, more cheerful than I'd ever seen him. He was actually whistling. Funerals affect people in different ways. As I reached for my copy of the *Bugle,* he asked, "Are you coming?" as if he meant to a party. I looked over at Jack. It was strange to see him at this hour. He must be doing double duty because Maggie and Paul were in court. For a second I considered skipping the funeral, but only for a second.

"I'll be there," I answered Jingles curtly. I said to Jack, "I started your story last night."

He stiffened and looked at me expectantly.

"It's good," I said firmly, thankful that I could be honest.

He relaxed.

Through the glass door I watched Jingles directing some bikers who were loading a beer keg onto a pickup. They must have borrowed or rented the truck just for the occasion. Bikes are not built for transporting big loads, as I'd discovered last night. The keg was followed by numerous cartons of hoagies, chips, pretzels, peanuts, and popcorn. The funeral meats? A vision of Sunny lying spread-eagle in that same parking lot rushed back to me. I turned to Jack. "Did you remember anything else from the party?"

He frowned. "Sunny had some words with that nonbiker guy."

"Stan?"

He nodded. "He was drinking some hard stuff from a regular drinking glass—and Sunny asked what it was. 'Bourbon,' he said. 'Wanna trade?' Sunny asked, and offered the guy his beer. The guy made a face and said, 'Never touch the stuff.' "

"Huh." What did that prove? That Stan was a beer snob. I was surprised Sunny hadn't snatched the bourbon from him. But I guess that would have been against the biker code—a breach of gentlemanly behavior. "Thanks, Jack. Keep thinking."

Speak of the devil. As I turned I bumped into Stan. He had stopped by the desk to pick up his paper. Coffee, doughnuts, and the *Bugle* were freebees supplied to guests by the Oakview Motor Lodge. I glanced at the headline:

BAYFIELD SON AWAITS VERDICT

Poor Mag. I bit my lip.

"Do you think he'll get the max?" Jack nodded at the headline.

I shrugged. The death penalty was still intact in New Jersey but seldom used. Life in prison with no parole was probably the worst he would draw. Bad enough, if you were the culprit's mother. I felt Stan hovering behind me, pretending to read his paper. "I hope not, for Maggie's sake," I answered Jack.

Stan cleared his throat. "You know this fellow?"

"He's the son of the people who own this motel," I said.

"No kidding!" His eyes grew round. "Wait'll I tell Fran." He hurried out.

Jack and I exchanged looks.

I hurried back to my room to get ready to go to the hospital. I wanted to be there in time for Bobby's release at 9:00 AM. I also wanted to apologize to him for my crankiness of the night before. As I rushed for my bike, I bumped into Mickey—the comic book artist—and had a brainstorm. "Hey, Mickey!" I grabbed his arm. "Are you busy this morning?"

"Nothin' special. Why?"

I told him.

"Sure." He grinned. "I'll get my stuff and meet you back here in five."

I smiled to myself. Maybe I could do one thing right today.

. . .

The boy was sitting on the bed, dressed in his shabby, ill-fitting clothes, his backpack at his side, ready to go.

"Hi, Bobby."

He looked up warily—checking my mood before smiling. Then he caught sight of Mickey—complete with leather jacket, jeans, boots, tattoos, long hair, and earrings—and his eyes started out of his head.

"I brought a friend to meet you."

"Hi, buddy." Mickey rolled forward.

Overcome with bashfulness (or fear), the boy was speechless.

"Mickey is a comic book artist," I said. "He's brought some stuff to show you."

Mickey sat down on the bed and opened the folder he was carrying. He pulled out a sheaf of papers. When Bobby caught sight of the drawings, all shyness vanished. "Wow!" He leaned forward. "These are great."

I left them, to attend to my other patients. When I came back an hour later, Mickey and Bobby were still sitting side by side on the bed. Mickey was drawing a superhero wrestling with a dragon. Bobby was watching, hypnotized. I hated to interrupt, but I'd glimpsed Bobby's father in the lobby, heading this way. I cleared my throat.

They glanced up.

"Your dad's on his way up, Bobby."

The boy's expression changed from sunlight to darkness. A second later, his father stepped into the room. Mr. Shoemaker's gaze slid over Mickey and me and settled on his son. "Let's go, boy."

Bobby jumped up and grabbed his backpack.

"Here." Mickey tore the drawing he had been working on from his pad and handed it to the boy.

With one eye fixed anxiously on his father, Bobby unzipped a pocket of his backpack and folded the drawing carefully inside.

"Come on. I don't have all day."

"Just a minute, Mr. Shoemaker. Before you go, I'd like a word with you." I moved out into the corridor, gesturing for him to follow. I handed him a sheet of printed instructions for changing his son's dressings and a prescription for the antibiotic the boy was to continue taking for five more days. Then I launched into the Bicycle Safety Lecture I'd prepared. Shoemaker shuffled impatiently, glancing at the door more than once, probably hoping his son would emerge and rescue him from this harridan. When I finally let him go, he charged back into the room, grabbed his son by the shoulder, and hurried him out. Bobby had time for no more than a quick glance over his shoulder at me. I smiled and waved him on.

"Nice kid," Mickey said.

"Yeah." I sighed. "Lousy home life, though."

The biker shook his long mane.

A couple of student nurses passed by, staring at Mickey's tattoos. When he winked, they giggled. In the elevator I thanked him for helping me out. "It meant a lot to Bobby," I said.

"Glad to do it. I know all about lousy home lives," he said.

I really was grateful. The least I could do was buy him a cup of coffee. Then I thought of the impression Mickey would make on my colleagues in the cafeteria. What the hell. I was ashamed of myself. "Would you like some coffee?"

"Sure."

Mickey had no compunctions about appearing in the hospital cafeteria. On the contrary, he reveled in the covert stares and whispers. That was part of the bikers' credo: don't give a damn what anybody thinks. "How did you get started with comic books?" I blurted.

"Doodling in school, when I shoulda been studying." He sounded very serious. "I had a big collection of comics at home, and in the beginning I just traced the heroes. Then I began to copy them. One day I decided to strike out on my own. I created one. His name was Devil Dan." He blushed.

"How old were you when you sold your first drawing?"

"Eighteen."

"Wow." I was no longer conscious of the other people in the room.

"Big day," he said proudly.

"When did you become a biker?"

"That same year, I became a hanger-on. Then a prospect."

"Prospect?"

"Yeah. That's when the members decide whether you've got the balls to be a member. You can't join the club officially until you're twenty-one."

"Do you have to pass a test?"

He snorted. "Nothing formal. But you've gotta prove you can handle yourself in a fight. Won't chicken out on the brothers. And that you're loyal."

"Righteous?"

"That's it."

"What about Jingles?"

"Huh?"

"Is he righteous?"

For a split second, Mickey hesitated. Then he said. "He's a member, ain't he?" He drained his cup and pushed back his chair. "I'll be going. Thanks for the cuppa."

"Wait." I had one more question. "What does that 'one percent' patch mean that some of the bikers wear?"

He gave me a slow smile. "They're special."

"How?"

He hesitated, then said, "Hell, it's no secret. They've taken a life. In some cases . . . more than one."

"And they're proud of it?"

"Sure. You can bet the fuckers deserved it." He laughed and took off.

I had barely registered Mickey's exit when his chair was filled by a colleague in a white coat.

"New boyfriend?" The young doctor grinned.

"Right, Carl."

"Just wondered. I heard about the murder at your motel. Are you helping the police again?"

Carl knew I'd had some part in clearing up the immigrant scam. "Not really."

"I heard the leader of that bike gang—"

"Club," I corrected him

"—is a suspect."

"We're all suspects, Carl. Everyone who was at the motel that night." I pushed back from the table. "I gotta run."

As I paid for the coffees, Detective Peck's card fell out of my wallet and I had my second brainstorm of the day. If Peck wanted me to share all my information with him, why shouldn't he share some of his info with me? Maybe he'd turned up something that could help me. I punched in his number on my cell phone.

"Peck speaking."

"Jo Banks."

"Any news?" He sounded eager.

"No, I'm stuck. I was hoping you could tell me something . . ."

Silence.

"Fair is fair. You tell me, I tell you. What about your rodenticide search? Did you turn up anything?"

More silence.

"If we're going to get to the bottom of this, we have to cooperate," I said.

I could hear the scales clinking as he weighed my suggestion. "We found that anyone could have access to those closets while the maids were cleaning," he said.

"You mean like guests?"

"That's right. The closets are unlocked—sometimes left wide open—until the maids put their equipment away for the day."

"Hmm."

"There was a box of rodenticide missing from the second floor closet."

My floor. "Huh."

"And by the way, if you want information, the state police are working on a plan to flush out that biker friend of yours."

My stomach did a backward flip.

He disconnected.

I shoved my cell into my backpack and ran for my bike. So far Bill Clinton's compartmentalization technique was working. I hadn't thought about Tom once. I was surprised he hadn't called, though. Maybe I should . . . *No.* He had no business spying on me! *He* should call! *Do you know how adolescent you sound? Shut up.* I forced my thoughts back into the Pi compartment. If they were going to flush him out, they must have some idea where he is! I punched in his cell number. It rang five times before voice mail broke in and told me to leave a message. I debated and decided against it. He probably just went for a walk. I'd try him again later.

As I tooled out of the hospital lot I caught sight of Chris Conner heading for the main entrance—a brightly wrapped package under one arm. I slowed and hailed him.

"Oh, hi. I'm going to see Bobby," he said.

"You're too late. He just left."

Chris looked crestfallen. "I bought him a catcher's mitt. Where does he live? I could take it to his house."

"Why not give it to me. I'll see that he gets it."

"Gee, thanks." He handed me the package.

"How're things going?" I asked.

He brightened. "OK. The Shoemaker complaint was reduced to a misdemeanor. My license was suspended for six weeks and I have to attend a driver safety class."

"That's great, Chris!"

I watched him head back to his car, where Ruth was waiting—in the driver's seat.

CHAPTER 28

As I dressed for the funeral, i.e., exchanged a pantsuit for jeans and a tee, an unpleasant thought hit me. *What if all this was a setup? What if Peck suspected that Pi would show up and the law would be lying in wait for him? Holy Mackerel! What an ass I am.* I had to warn Pi. I punched his number on my room phone. *Damn.* Still no answer. He could be already on his way. In remote south Jersey there were dead pockets where cell phones often didn't work. My stomach contracted. Would Pi show up in disguise? What if I didn't recognize him? Grabbing my leather jacket and helmet, I took off.

Except for Pi's description of Freddy's funeral, I wasn't sure what to expect. Having glimpsed the funeral meats, I feared a repeat of the blast in the parking lot. This time I was determined not to drink or get involved. I was going for one reason. To act as eyes and ears for Pi, to be alert to anything that would help find Sunny's murderer, and—even more important—to keep an eye out for any law enforcers who might be looking for him.

As I neared the Potter place, I saw the bikes lined up along both sides of the road. There were more bikes than the dozen belonging to the Satan's Apostles—there must have been at least fifty. How had they gotten wind of this so quickly? Extrasensory perception? Cell phones, more likely. Before parking, I trundled between the two rows, searching for Pi's bike with its distinctive logo—a dark pony nestled in a light circle. Not here. Had he disguised that, too? I turned and pulled in behind the last bike, leaving plenty of room in front, in case I had to make a quick exit. When I removed my helmet, the cacophony of sound burst on me from the woods. Judas Priest at top volume, mixed with the familiar yips and yodels of the boys. I wondered what the deer were thinking. Or had they already left for Alaska?

I threaded my way through the trees toward the melee, snapping dead branches with my boots. I might have been tiptoeing barefoot across a freshly mowed lawn for all the noise I made. It was completely drowned out by the noise beyond. It was hard to imagine anyone lying quietly there. Even a corpse. But—hey—was this really any different from a Catholic wake? They partied around the deceased at those, too. Or an African-American funeral, where people rose one after the other, loudly venting their emotions. It wasn't uncommon to bury your grief in booze or indulge in a cathartic display before giving your friends or relatives to the ground. Only Episcopalians (and maybe Quakers) resisted these natural impulses. *Closure* was the current clinical term for such time-honored traditions. Bikers' way of dealing with death and loss was just a little more exuberant than others'. As I emerged into the clearing, I quickly scanned the faces for Pi. Not here. Maybe he'd wised up at the last minute and taken my advice to stay away. As I stood in the shadow of a big sycamore, Mickey spied me.

"Yo, Doc!" All eyes turned on me. "Have a beer?" He pointed to the dripping keg invitingly.

Out of the corner of my eye, I glimpsed the dark hole the bikers had prepared for Sunny. On the picnic table (borrowed, along with two benches, from the motel) lay a pine box topped with a giant wreath. The flowers—black and white tulips, the colors of the club—were arranged in the shape of their logo, a white skull in a black oval, with a red tulip projecting from the right eye socket to indicate that a brother had died. As I drew nearer I saw that under the wreath, the coffin was open. Despite my resolution, I accepted a paper cup full of beer from Mickey. No way was I getting through this sober.

"Nice of you to come, Doc," Honey was saying.

"The service hasn't started yet," Mickey assured me. "The minister's late."

"Minister?"

"Well—almost a minister," Mickey amended. "He went to seminary, but didn't take orders."

"Who?"

"Jingles."

My face must have been a picture, because all the boys nearby went, "Haw! Haw! Haw!"

I noticed a few other females among the crowd. Some were *old ladies*, the name given to wives or steady girlfriends of the bikers, who were untouchable according to the biker code. But one or two fell into another category called *mamas*, women who hung around the club and were used by the members any time they felt the urge.

As I gulped my beer I saw a tall figure emerging from the woods. Clad in black leather from head to foot, with his scrawny neck, stringy hair, and goatee, clutching a Bible, Jingles resembled one of those forbidding clerics from Puritan days, described so vividly by Hawthorne—or was it Melville? For the first time, I noticed the 1 percent patch on his sleeve. At a nod from the "minister" someone turned down the boom box a few decibels, the boys lowered their yips and yodels a few notches, and something like a semihush fell over the glade. For the moment, at least, Jingles was in charge.

I felt a rush of anger. I almost wished Pi *would* show up and get rid of this imposter.

Jingles walked to the head of the grave. At a signal, six bikers went to the picnic table and raised the coffin slowly to their shoulders. With deliberate steps, they moved forward. Amid grunts and sighs, they lowered the box into the hole. Despite their muscle and girth, a corpse is a deadweight (no pun intended) and makes the already heavy box harder to lift, carry, and lower. Once the box had settled, Jingles gestured for the rest of us to come forward. Obediently we arranged ourselves around the edge of the grave. Someone leaped in and reopened the coffin. I tried to avert my gaze, but it was drawn downward against my will. Sunny lay in full biker regalia, eyes closed, surrounded by memorabilia that his friends must have added before I arrived. Beer mugs decorated with nude females, girlie magazines, and calendars—remembrances of Sunny's overactive sex life. Trinkets from his bike—a red taillight, a photo of the bike, and his saddlebag—also nestled there. The bike itself would go to the next "prospect" who couldn't afford one. Pi had told me that bikes were too valuable to be buried with their owners except in rare cases such as Freddy's.

"Let's pray," Jingles said.

One by one the bikers bowed their heads.

Jingles turned his face upward to the lofty new spring leaves and offered a strange prayer. I can only remember bits and pieces: "To our beloved brother . . . we wish you joy on your last ride. . . . May it be a dream run . . . at top speed . . . with a brisk wind at your back . . . a clear sky overhead . . . with no bumps or detours. Amen."

"Amen," the bikers echoed in unison.

For some reason, this last Amen, uttered by so many rumbling male voices, moved me. It sounded genuine.

A wiry biker, who I hadn't seen before, darted around the periphery of the grave handing out paper cups full of beer to anyone who didn't have one, including me. When everyone was supplied, Jingles quoted the traditional ". . . ashes to ashes, dust to dust." While I waited for him to reach down for a handful of earth to throw on the coffin, the bikers began to whoop and holler and toss their beer into the grave. As I stood aghast, still holding my cup, a hand reached around me from behind, grabbed it, and tossed its contents into the hole. "When in Rome . . ." a voice whispered in my ear.

I spun around to see a female biker who definitely fell into the Mama category. Her face was framed by silvery blond hair, her mouth was heavily made up, and her boobs were the size of cantaloupes. Her eyes were hidden by the visor of her helmet. As I stared, she raised the visor and winked.

Under ordinary circumstances I would have slugged him, but now was not the time or the place to call attention to Pi. I turned back to the grave, hoping the solemnity of the view would cure my fit of the giggles.

I found the coffin closed and Jingles in the midst of another prayer. Actually, it was a poem some biker had written about the joys of the biker life. I caught only the last two lines:

The pull of the horizon keeps us on the move,
There is no stronger love than the love of the open road . . .

Someone began to sing "O God Our Help in Ages Past," but it quickly turned into Nine Inch Nails and suddenly the place was swinging. Once the deceased was disposed of, the real partying began. Music was turned up to full strength; food was broken out— along with more booze, pot, and "crank" (methamphetamine). No cocaine or heroin, though. Pi had told me hard drugs were taboo in his club. Anyone caught injecting was thrown out. And I didn't see anybody shooting up. I went to look for Pi.

CHAPTER 29

On closer inspection, I saw that Pi's silvery blond locks had been cleverly crafted from my old friend—phragmites. Those silvery tassels resembled the work of the most creative New York hairstylist. Someone's old lady had loaned him the makeup, he told me. And his boobs were a pair of rolled-up biker socks. "Wanna feel?" When I refused this offer, Pi melted into the crowd.

The party continued along the usual lines. It seemed to be a rerun of the parking lot gala—with one addition: the boys swinging their shovels, filling in the grave. This time I was determined to go easy on the booze. I managed to swallow half a hoagie and a handful of peanuts without the aid of liquid refreshment. For whatever reason, the boys didn't hassle me. Maybe after Sunny died they considered me bad news or bad luck. Anyway, I was left pretty much to myself, and while they caroused around me I used the time to observe them, looking for anything suspicious that might give me a clue to the big question: who killed Sunny.

At one point a bunch of the boys formed a tableau, draped around the picnic table, stuffing their faces. Pi was in the center. For a brief moment, with their long hair and beards, I was reminded of Leonardo's *Last Supper*. But the image faded quickly when Jingles leaped onto the table and began dancing—a combination of Irish jig and Elvis gyrations. Jingles certainly was the star of the show today.

The other boys clapped and hollered, egging him on until he toppled off the table to the ground.

I also kept a careful watch on the woods for any sign of the law. Now and then I even walked back to the road to check things out. Once a farmer rumbled by on his tractor, cast a quizzical look at the woods, and shook his head. Another time a bunch of rednecks in a pickup slowed, eyeballed the string of bikes hungrily, and moved on.

By five o'clock the sun was low, the grave had been transformed from a cavity to a mound, and everyone was drunk—except me. Apparently Peck had been true to his word and kept the cops away. I glanced over at Pi. With a jolt, I recognized him easily. His silver wig was askew, his lipstick had worn away, and his boobs had slipped to his waist. I was about to warn him when a ray from the dying sun glinted on something bright among the trees behind Pi. A metal badge attached to a gray uniform. I sprinted forward, but Jingles jostled me out of the way. He was jigging and singing, still making a damn fool of himself, as he headed toward Pi. When he reached Pi, he clasped him in one of those brotherly bear hugs and planted a sloppy kiss on his lips. I felt a wave of nausea and rushed over to Pi. But when I told him about the trooper, he just smiled. "After three days in that fuckin' marsh, state prison would look good," he said. "At least there ain't no mosquitoes!"

"Shut up, Pi. You're drunk," I whispered urgently. "I don't think he's seen you yet. Take my bike." I pushed my bike keys into his hand.

He stared at the keys as if they were contaminated. "That sissy— Linus?"

"It's parked three from the end on the left. Give me *your* keys and I'll meet you back at the shack." As I talked I was pushing him out of the clearing—through the trees, toward the road.

"You jush wanna ride my hog. . . ." He looked at me accusingly.

"Your keys!" I hissed.

He reached in his pocket and tossed them at me.

In a final burst of genius, I tore off my helmet and jacket and shoved them at him. "Now give me yours!"

"Jesus, you want my clothes, too?" Reluctantly he handed me his vest.

I flipped off his helmet and placed it on my head. It was a little loose. I adjusted the strap. "And you'd better fix your boobs," I hissed after him.

As I watched him stumble drunkenly toward the road, I had a terrible thought—*What if he kills himself? Or somebody else?* Too late to worry about that. I started for his bike and suddenly realized he hadn't told me where it was. Shit. I'd have to hunt for it. I glanced over my shoulder and saw not one but two gray uniforms. I was relieved to see they were converging on *me*, not Pi. I ran down the row of bikes glancing from side to side at the logos. Thank god, Pi's was the most distinctive and I spotted it easily. Behind me, I recognized the sound of my motor starting up. A moment later, Pi rumbled past me into the setting sun. I glanced back at the troopers. They had changed course, heading away from me, toward their car. They had parked it off the road in some bushes—a halfhearted attempt to hide it. I kick-started the Harley (it almost took my leg off!) and headed east, the opposite direction from Pi. They couldn't chase both of us! I was banking on their recognizing Pi's tag number and choosing me. Right away I felt the surge of power under me. I had only a few seconds' head start, but I intended to make the most of them. I twisted the throttle up to the max.

I heard the troopers make a screeching U-turn and sighed with relief. They were coming after me. The hog was much bigger and heavier than my own bike and took some getting used to. Despite the circumstances, I thrilled to my first ride on a Harley—the speed, the power, the sound. In seconds, I was out of their sight. I skimmed past a tractor-trailer that was humming along, minding its own business. The driver's curses were lost on the wind.

I led the law a merry chase, bumping over country roads, diving through rows of new green corn, twisting around the ragged shores of Stow Creek. At Stow Creek Landing, I came to a dead stop and waited for them to catch up. While I waited, I inhaled slowly and deeply, willing myself to relax. By the time I heard the troopers draw up behind me, I was ready for them. They leaped out of the car, guns drawn. Although I was facing the creek, I could see them in my side mirrors. Their expressions, under their broad-brimmed hats, were smug. They had cornered their prey.

I turned and slowly lifted my visor.

"What the fuck?" squawked the lead officer. The other stood gaping.

"Careful," I said with a smile. "Ladies present."

CHAPTER 30

My triumph was short-lived. They were on me in a split second. They didn't touch me. I'll give them that. But they were in my face, their anger tangible, like hot flashes. They had not enjoyed the ride over ruts and gullies, fields and ditches, at ninety miles an hour, rattling around in their car like a pair of dice in a cup. Patrol cars are not bikes. They demanded to know what I was doing riding Pi's bike. Why I was wearing his helmet and colors. Where he was. And . . . that I take them to him.

I sat, as if soldered to the bike seat, facing the creek.

"We can arrest you for bike theft," Trooper #1 said.

"And for aiding and abetting a murder suspect," said Trooper #2.

That did it. I gave a horselaugh. "On what evidence?"

"Leaving the scene of a crime," said #1.

"Bullshit. He never knew there *was* a crime!" I cried.

Their expressions were a mix of pity and incredulity. Trooper #2 said, "Come on, Doc; you're a bright girl. You know better than that."

I felt my own anger thudding in my ears. I refused to speak again.

"You'd better come back with us to headquarters," #1 said. "You lead, we'll follow—unless you want to take us to Pi, that is."

I remained mute.

"To headquarters, then. And keep that speedometer under fifty," he warned.

There were two of them and they were armed. I pressed the kick-start, turned the bike around, and paused a few yards ahead of the patrol car. When they were inside, they beeped their horn. I set off at thirty-five miles an hour, deciding to have a little more fun with them. They beeped angrily at my pace. I slowed to twenty-five. Trooper #1 leaned on the horn. I went back to thirty-five. Finally, tired of playing games, I sped up to fifty.

Dusk had settled; blue shadows had gathered; the air had cooled. Phragmites rose on either side giving the illusion that we were traveling down a corridor between two solid walls. But I knew they weren't solid; phrags were light, hollow reeds—easily bendable. Breakable. I spied a spot where they had been bent and broken by some farm vehicle in the recent past. On impulse, I accelerated and made a sharp right turn. I tore through the wall of stalks as if it were tissue paper and raced across a field toward a grove of trees. Decelerating, I wriggled the hog between the trees and came out on the other side, ending up on Snakeskin Road, a road I knew well. A glance over my shoulder revealed an empty landscape. Home free. I made another right and headed for the fisherman's shack and the state of Delaware.

When I ground to a halt in front of the shack, it was almost dark. I could barely make out Pi's bulk draped over a wicker chair on the porch. The red tip of a cigarette glowed in one hand and I was sure he was cradling a beer in the other.

"You look comfy," I said, fuming.

"I patched the screens," he said proudly. Bug-protected and supplied with beer—he was serene.

"They're coming for you, Pi. They followed me. I gave them the slip, but it won't be long before they pick up my trail."

"Shit, man, I thought you said this was a safe house," he said, but he still seemed unperturbed.

"It is. But we have to explain that to them."

"You explain it. I'm just an innocent bystander."

I dismounted and glanced around. "Where's Linus?"

"Back of the house."

I pushed open the screen door and stepped onto the porch.

"Shut the fuckin' door! You're lettin' the mosquitoes in!"

"*Sorree!*" It was the first real sign of alarm he'd shown all day. I shut the door and hooked it.

"Wanna beer?"

"Sure." I slumped into a wicker rocker. All my bones ached. The Harley is a fast ride, but not always a smooth one. He handed me a cold can. "How come it's still cold?"

"I dunked it in the bay," he said, as if *he'd* thought of it.

"Will wonders never cease? When did you fix the screens?"

"This morning, before the funeral."

He puffed and I rocked in companionable silence—a brother and sister team, taking a break together.

I sat up.

"What's the matter?"

"Hush." I heard the throb of a car approaching. "Get inside!" I ordered.

He had barely disappeared inside the house when headlight beams illuminated the porch and me, as if I were on stage. I resisted the urge to go into my song and dance routine.

The car stopped and two officers leaped out, guns drawn. Déjà vu. Assheads. But they scared me. I went and stood at the screen door.

"You're under arrest!" Officer #1 shouted.

"You can't arrest me," I said, carefully enunciating every sylla-ble. "I'm out of your jurisdiction."

Their faces, lit from below by the headlights they had left on, resembled Halloween masks. "And I'm The Jolly Green Giant," Officer #1 sneered.

"Check your map, Officer. You're no longer in Jersey. This is Delaware." I held my ground.

He turned to his buddy for support, but Officer #2 looked dis-concerted.

"If you don't have a map, I can give you one," I offered. Then remembered that it was tucked in my saddlebag. As they continued to hesitate, I gained confidence and added, "Or maybe you should call headquarters and check my information out."

Officer #1 started toward me.

I glanced at the pathetic hook that held the screen door shut and swallowed. Forcing a tone of authority, I let them have my final shot: "You'd better check this out before you make fools of yourselves with your superior officers."

Officer #1 hesitated.

"We might as well call," #2 muttered.

Officer #1 took out his cell and punched in a number. I heard him identify himself, describe his location, and repeat what I had just told him. I held my breath. Before I had to draw another, Trooper #1 got his answer. "No kidding," he said, his face registering disbelief. He disconnected.

"We'll be back," he promised, and gestured for his buddy to get in the car.

They spun off in a spray of sand and gravel. When their taillights had disappeared, I called to Pi. "You can come out now."

He came out and treated me to one of his rib-crushing bear hugs, but no kiss. "You were good," he said. "Real good. You got rid of them without letting in one skeeter."

I collapsed in the rocker, laughing with relief, and reached for my beer.

"Now give me back my colors," he ordered.

I stripped off his vest.

He grabbed it and clutched it to his chest.

"Poor baby, did you miss your security blanket?" I settled back in my chair and picked up my beer again. It was warm.

He sat cross-legged on the floor, lit another Marlboro, and asked, "How'd you like my hog?"

I shrugged, nonchalant. "It was OK."

"You're full of shit."

"How'd you like my baby?"

He didn't deign to answer.

The remains of Pi's wig lay on the floor, where he must have tossed it when he came in. I picked it up and examined it. It was the work of an artist. He had cut two sets of slender phragmites and woven them painstakingly together at the top—like the Lenapes had woven their mats over three hundred years ago. He must have soaked the reeds in the bay first, to make them pliable. When he put the wig on, the tassels hung down on either side of his face in clusters, resembling silvery locks.

"It almost fooled you, didn't it?" he said with a note of pride.

I caressed the tassels gently. "You can always become a hairstylist when you get tired of biking." I laid the wig aside.

"Tired of biking?" He laughed and stretched. "That'll be the same day I get tired of breathing."

We sat in silence for a while, sipping and puffing, recovering from the troopers' house call.

"Now what?" Pi said finally, crushing out his butt.

"We have a reprieve, that's all. Time for me to ask some more questions." I rose. "Speaking of which, I'd better get going." I unhooked the screen door.

"Why don't you get that boyfriend of yours to help?" he said. "He seemed pretty smart." Had he forgiven Tom for lopping off Sunny's ear? Or, in the light of subsequent events, had that insult paled in significance?

"We're not exactly close these days," I confessed.

"What d'ya mean?"

"He saw a certain biker embracing me."

"Oh, shit."

As I opened the door, he said, "Jo."

"I won't let in any damned mosquitoes," I said irritably.

"If you don't come up with something in the next twenty-four hours . . . I'm outta here." He was dead serious.

"But—"

"I can't stick around with those fuckin' cops breathing down my neck."

I glanced at my watch. A little past eight. It felt more like midnight. It had been a long day. That meant the police and I had only the rest of tonight and tomorrow to find Sunny's murderer.

"Sleep tight." I said.

CHAPTER 31

On the way home, despite Pi's ultimatum and the pressure to concentrate solely on Sunny's murder, my compartmentalization technique broke down momentarily. It had served me well all day, but as I rode through the darkness, Tom crept through a crack in my brain. I had expected him to call by now. My feelings for Pi were so obviously platonic, it was hard for me to believe Tom was jealous. Maybe I'd better call him and explain after all. . . .

But when I entered the lobby of the motel, all thoughts of Tom and Pi were blown away. Jack was at his post, perusing a late edition of the *Bayside Bugle*. Late edition? the *Bugle* never had more than one edition.

BAYFIELD SON GUILTY: DEATH PENALTY

"Ohmygod!"
Jack lowered his paper.
"Where is Mag?"
"Home."
As I flew out of the lobby, I passed Fran and Stan on the sofa, huddled over a copy of the *Bugle*, lapping up every word.

. . .

In front of the Nelson house, a long line of cars trailed up and down both sides of the road. I pulled up to the end of one line and parked. Through the lighted front window of the small ranch house I glimpsed what at first glance looked like a party—people moving to and fro, standing in clusters, eating and drinking, As I drew closer, I saw their expressions. This was no party. Every face was sober and drawn, and I knew before I entered the voices would be subdued and there would be no laughter.

I tried the door. According to country custom, it was unlocked. I stepped inside. A few heads turned toward me and nodded greetings, but no one smiled. I recognized most of the guests—friends, neighbors, and patients, in some cases embodying all three in one.

"Can I get you some coffee or tea, Jo?" Polly came up. Polly was Maggie's younger sister. She taught art at the local grammar school. We had met once before, and when I discovered she loved New York, we'd really hit it off. We had even planned a trip to Manhattan together.

"No, thanks, Polly. Where's Mag?"

"In back." She lowered her voice. "Lying down."

"How's she taking it?"

She shook her head.

"And Paul?"

"Over there."

I looked where she nodded. Paul was surrounded by a bunch of his farmer and fishermen friends. He had aged ten years in a day. I took a sharp breath. Standing behind Paul was Tom. He glanced up, and I know he saw me. But he looked quickly away.

The snatches of conversation that I overheard centered on such topics as fish ("How's the shad running?" "Fair to middlin'") and crops ("Start your plantin' yet?" and "Tractor's bein' repaired . . .") No one dared touch on the reason we were all there.

I edged through the throng toward the back of the house. The hall was dark except for a single strand of light leaking from a half-open door.

I knocked.

"Who is it?"

Barely recognizing the feeble voice, I went in.

Maggie was curled on the bed in a fetal position, a comforter tucked around her, although the night was mild. A cup of untouched tea was cooling on the table beside her. I sat on the end of the bed and reached for her hand. It was cold and limp.

After her initial recognition, she closed her eyes again.

"Mag, listen. He'll appeal. It will take years to go through the courts. The sentence might be overturned."

No answer.

"He has his new faith. That'll help him through this," I added desperately.

Her eyes opened.

"He told me he didn't care about the sentence," I said. "All he wanted—and these are his very words—was 'to make it up with my parents.'"

She raised her head, fixing her gaze on me. "He said that?"

I nodded.

"You never told me that," she snapped.

Startled by her unexpected anger, I felt a twinge of guilt. In all the furor over the bikers, I'd neglected to transmit this bit of information.

"Sorry," I said. "I forgot."

"Forgot?" She drew herself up, eyes flashing. "If I'd known that, it would have made this terrible day a little easier."

"I'm really sorry, Mag," I repeated.

With a sigh, she sank back against the pillows. "Go away, Jo. Just go away." She closed her eyes again.

"Mag, I'm really sorry. Things were so upset with that biker's death, and the funeral, and—"

"Oh, you and those bikers. I don't know what you see in them. Besides, you talked to Nick long before that biker died." She cast me another accusatory look. "I'd thought better of you, Jo."

Her words stung. She lay still, eyes closed. I watched her for a while. When her breathing became regular, I tiptoed out.

The living room was still crowded and had grown a little noisier.

I noticed that the tea and coffee cups had been replaced by paper cups, and I caught sight of a whiskey bottle being passed around. Paul was holding a paper cup and his face had regained some of its natural color. Thank god for small solaces. I scanned the room for Tom. I caught his eye. His gaze sliced through me like a knife through baloney at a cold-cut counter. The blood rose to my face and I escaped through the front door.

As I mounted my bike, under the brilliant night sky, I paused to take stock. A few hours ago, I'd felt proud of myself—the way I'd handled those troopers. Now I felt like the lowliest worm. I glanced up at the vast universe glittering overhead and told myself: *What does it matter? In a nanosecond, via astronomical time, all the players in this little drama will be dust.* This usually worked.

Not tonight.

I fell into bed. Although exhausted, I knew the minute I turned out the light demons from the past few days would pop out and plague me. In a desperate attempt to fend them off, I reached for Jack's manuscript. It lay on the floor where I had left it the night before.

I began to read and found myself wanting to read more. No doubt about it. Jack had a way with words. However, sleep overtook me. I would finish it tomorrow.

SATURDAY

CHAPTER 32

I woke with a panicky feeling, as if something or someone was chasing me and time was running out. Then I remembered Pi's ultimatum. If some evidence of Sunny's real killer wasn't found by eight o'clock tonight, he would cop out and take off for points west and probably be caught and arrested for a crime he didn't commit. This knowledge had barely sunk in when the phone rang. Tom? I snatched up the receiver.

"Hi, Jo." Becca.

"Uh . . ." I grunted.

"Are you still mad at me?"

With an effort I remembered the last time I had seen Becca. I'd been in a bad mood. I said quickly, "No. Not at all."

"Good, 'cause I'm coming over."

"Now?" I cast a sleepy glance at my digital alarm clock. "It's not even seven."

"I gotta talk to you." Her tone was urgent. "It's about Bobby."

"What about Bobby?" I was fully awake.

"He came to school yesterday with a black eye."

I sat up. "You're kidding." A black eye meant a blow to the head. This to a kid recovering from a severe concussion. "I'll meet you at the Blue Arrow. We'll have pancakes—my treat!"

I jumped out of bed and rushed through my morning ablutions.

. . .

Between mouthfuls of blueberry pancakes, bacon, and a double order of orange juice, Becca told me all she knew about Bobby's black eye. It was frustratingly little. He'd shown up for class on Friday morning with his left eye swollen half-shut and the skin around his eye stained varying shades of blue and purple. The homeroom teacher had called him over and they had a whispered conference. Or rather, the teacher whispered while Bobby stood silent, occasionally shaking his head. The teacher announced to the class that she had to leave for a few minutes and asked them to please behave themselves until she got back. Then she and Bobby left.

"Shit!"

Becca laughed. "You've been hangin' out with those bikers too much."

"Sorry." I flushed. "Want some more pancakes?"

"No, thanks." She patted her usually flat tummy, which now resembled a small bowling ball.

"You have syrup on your chin." I drained my second cup of coffee. I'd had no appetite for anything more solid.

She wiped her chin. "So what are we going to do?"

I looked away. What I'd like to do was ride over to Bobby's house and throttle his father. But I had enough sense to know that wouldn't solve anything and might hurt the boy further. "I don't know," I said slowly. "Let me think about it. What was the name of that teacher?"

"Mrs. Dalton."

"For a start, I'll give Mrs. Dalton a call, and we'll go on from there."

Becca looked disappointed. She'd expected more immediate action. "Can't we go beat him up?"

I grinned. As usual, Becca and I were on the same wavelength. "I wish," I said. "But that wouldn't do any good. And it would get us into trouble."

Becca was quiet, stirring a microscopic piece of bacon in a pool of syrup with her fork. "How can a man treat his own son like that?" The honest wonder in her voice made me look up. Her pale forehead under its fringe of rusty bangs was puckered in disbelief. I reached over and rubbed her head.

"Some people can be lousy," I said. "But most people are nice."

She made an inarticulate sound—something between a retch and a groan, conveying her opinion of my answer.

I caught myself up short. I had been lying so much lately, now I was even lying to Becca. "Sorry, Bec. There *are* evil people in the world. People who get a bang out of hurting others. Sadists, they're called. This is a fact. That's one of the reasons we have policemen and courts, and juries and jails. Some of these people can be helped. Rehabilitated. But not all." I thought of Nick. Could he be saved? "Some are evil to the core. Nothing will change them and they have to be put in jail."

I signaled to the waitress for more coffee. I needed more fuel to continue my lecture. "And evil people are not always obvious. You know—dressed in black with horns and cloven feet, carrying pitchforks. Sometimes they come in the shape of a beautiful woman or a charming man, just as some beautiful flowers are poisonous. . . ."

"My aunt is beautiful—so was my mother."

"And neither of them is or was evil. All I'm saying is—sometimes bad people come in nice packages and are very charming. The other side of the coin is—good people can put us off with their bad appearance."

"Like the bikers?"

"Right. Despite their tattoos, earrings, beards, bad language, many of them are OK. Not all. . . ." Which reminded me, I had to wrap this up and get back to the motel. "As you grow older, have more experience, you get a sixth sense about people."

"Like you?" Becca grinned wickedly.

"Yeah. But even at my advanced age, I sometimes make mistakes." I wondered what mistakes I was making now.

"But Bobby is such a nice kid. . . ." She still didn't get it.

"Of course he is. Some people just get a kick out of hurting people—nice people, not nice people, even their own children." I was on a truth roll now and refused to back down—to sugarcoat this. I told her a story a judge had told me. "There was once a man who took out life insurance on his five-year-old son, then killed him, and collected. Because he got away with it, he took out a policy on his three-year-old daughter and killed her, too. But this time they caught him. The judge looked at me and said, 'What do you do with a person like that?' I couldn't answer him."

Becca gave me a grave look. She was beginning to understand.

Thoughts of Pi, Mag, and Tom were scratching at the door of the Bobby compartment. "I have to get back," I said. I left a big tip and headed for the cashier.

True to my word, as soon as I got back to my room, I called Mrs. Dalton. Becca sprawled on my bed and listened intently to my side of the conversation. Mrs. Dalton told me she had been unable to get anything out of Bobby and his parents' phone was disconnected, "Probably because they hadn't paid the bill," she confided. She had reported all this to the principal yesterday. He told her he would inform the school board, who would study the matter and decide whether to turn the case over to the county authorities. *Bureaucratic bullshit.* I held my tongue, but it wasn't easy. The county would send a caseworker out to see if the boy should be placed in foster care.

I stifled a groan. I knew all about foster care. When I was an intern at Bellevue, the caseworkers used to entertain us with horror stories. Sometimes the kids were better off with their natural parents. I listened patiently until Mrs. Dalton ran out of steam, thanked her, and hung up.

"Now what?" Becca had read my expression and knew the conversation had not been satisfactory.

"Now you go home and I go to work. There's nothing more we can do till Monday, when I can talk to the county authorities."

"But Bobby may be dead by then!" She was outraged.

"That's very unlikely. This is the first time you've seen him with any bruises, isn't it?"

She nodded.

"We have to take some risk."

"Can't we ride over and see him?"

I thought about that and decided in the negative. I was Bobby's physician and there were certain professional rules that had to be observed, such as not chasing after a patient—waiting until he called you. "*I* can't," I said, "but I guess you could. Just ride over and say you dropped by to see how Bobby is."

"OK." Becca was eager.

I walked her out to the parking lot. As she got on her bike, I warned, "If you see something you don't like, Becca, *don't do anything*. Call me on your cell phone. Promise?"

She nodded. Then she tapped my arm. "There's that guy whose wife was yelling in the room next to yours."

I followed her gaze and saw Stan putting a suitcase in the trunk of his car. "How did you know what he looked like?" I asked.

"When I heard him leave, I poked my head out and saw him."

As we watched, Fran appeared around the side of the car wearing her usual uniform—a too-tight tank top, a pair of too-short short shorts, and sandals. She threw a tote bag into the trunk and sashayed back to the passenger seat. Seems they were checking out. Had Fran had her fill of bikers? Or had Stan? I wondered if Peck had given them permission to leave. Stan slammed the trunk lid shut and I saw their tag. UR4ME. Cute. Her brainstorm, no doubt. Was the message for her husband or any dude who happened to be on her tail?

Becca pedaled away with a wave as Stan edged his car out of the lot.

CHAPTER 33

The bikers loitered in the lobby and parking lot, pacing and snarling like caged animals. How much longer would Peck be able to keep them here? I wondered. Paul was at the front desk reading the paper. The headline was smaller today but still prominent:

NELSON FILES APPEAL

"How's Mag?" I asked.

He lowered the paper and shook his head.

"What about you?" I ventured. This was the first time I'd spoken to him since our tiff.

To my relief, he gave a shaky smile. "I'll live."

"Is there *anything* I can do?" I asked.

"Go see her."

"She wasn't too happy to see me last night." I told him what Nick had said about wanting to make it up to his parents and how I'd forgotten to tell Maggie.

He shrugged. "Take her something," he said finally. "Some fruit. A pie. Anything. She won't eat it, but she'll appreciate it. And maybe she'll talk to you. She needs to talk."

I was amazed at the transformation in this man. Now it was he who was showing concern for Maggie, giving advice to me. I nodded, stowing my paper under my arm.

"You take care of yourself," I advised earnestly. "Be sure to eat properly and get enough sleep."

"Thanks, Doctor." His smile was a little less shaky.

In the hall outside my room, Marie was vacuuming. When she saw me she turned off the machine. "They're gone!" she said gleefully, nodding at the room next to mine.

"I know. I saw them leave."

"But it'll probably take me all day to clean that pigsty." A frown replaced her smile.

"Well, once it's done it's done," I said unhelpfully.

"Any leads on that dead biker?" she asked.

I shook my head.

"Maybe it was an outsider."

I stared.

"I mean, not one of the bikers staying here. There were a lot of people at that party. Who knows where they came from."

"You're right." I slipped my key in my lock. (They still used real keys at the Oakview Motor Lodge.) "Thanks, Marie."

Once inside, I slumped on the bed, my head in my hands. *What's wrong with me?* Marie's simple suggestion made more sense than anything I'd come up with for days. Maybe it was an outsider. One of those chicks they'd brought in from Wildwood for example. Maybe one of them had a history with Sunny. How could I find out? *Talk to the bikers, Dork!* But would they talk to me? *Sure they will.* They're as anxious to get this thing solved as you are, so they can get the hell out of here. I got up and made myself some sludge, i.e., instant coffee mixed with warm tap water. If you drink it quickly, it's not bad and it does the trick. I felt the effects of the caffeine almost instantly. Recharged, I set out in search of bikers.

As I passed Stan and Fran's former domicile, the door was open and I heard Marie cleaning and cussing inside. She had set two overflowing trash baskets out in the hall. Dirty Kleenex, soiled paper towels, a squeezed-out toothpaste tube. Why was other people's trash so much more gross than your own? And bourbon bottles. Six empties lined up against the wall.

CHAPTER 34

When I trudged into the lobby there wasn't a biker in sight. Best laid plans and all that.

"They went for a run," Paul said.

I grunted. Waiting was the hardest part. I almost regretted not having Saturday office hours. Even seeing Mrs. Lockweed would be better than facing these empty hours.

"Why don't you go see Mag?" Paul prodded again. "I'm stuck here till five and she's all alone."

"Good idea," I said, not knowing if it was or not. But it was an opportunity to atone for my recent neglect.

At a roadside stand near the motel, I bought a bunch of fresh asparagus and some wild flowers. It was nice to see these stands displaying goods again. All winter they had stood bleak and bare. Asparagus was the first to show up in May. June brought the strawberries. Then the vegetables started to trickle in. Peas and string beans first, then the lettuce, cucumbers, and carrots. And finally in August, the big blast: Jersey corn and tomatoes. My mouth watered just thinking about them.

The flowers would look better in a vase, I decided. (Or was I just putting off this visit?) Whatever. I stopped in the lobby and headed for the cupboard under the front desk. This cupboard was a catchall for odds and ends; the sign-in book, extra keys, phone books, and a vase or two for those occasional times when Maggie felt inspired to put flowers on the desk. No one was on duty. Paul must have stepped out for a minute. I rummaged inside, feeling in the dark, until I touched something smooth. I pulled it out. Not a vase, but a beer bottle. I was about to toss it, when something stopped me. Giving the bottle a second glance, I noticed it wasn't dusty and there was still an inch of liquid in the bottom. Holding it gingerly by the neck, I saw some sediment floating in the liquid. I don't know what possessed me. Maybe that shot of caffeine. But I set the bottle carefully on the desk, reached for my cell, and called Peck.

When he recognized my voice, he said angrily, "You led my boys on a merry chase!"

"And you broke your promise," I snapped. " 'No police at the funeral,' you said."

"Well . . . I had my reasons."

I held my tongue only because I was about to ask for a favor. I told him about the beer bottle and asked if he'd check it for prints. His opinion of my hunch was close to zero, but he told me to bring the bottle into the lab.

"Better test the contents, too," I said. "There's a small liquid residue."

"Sure, Doc. Whatever you say. Anything else we can do for you? How about a round-trip ticket to Disney World?"

"I'm not Mickey Mousing you!" I snapped.

He actually laughed.

"How long will it take for a report?" I was thinking of Pi's ultimatum.

"They should have it before closing. The lab shuts down at five. But don't get your hopes up."

I wrapped the bottle carefully in a paper towel, tucked it upright in my saddlebag to protect the contents, and broke the speed limit riding to Bridgeton. Fortunately none of my trooper buddies were around. As I came out of the police lab, I heard the courthouse clock striking eleven. Only nine hours before Pi took off and ruined his life for good. I sped back to the motel, hoping some bikers might have returned and

I could ask them about those other outsiders, before I went to see Maggie. It would be a mistake to pin all my hopes on one beer bottle.

There wasn't a single bike or biker in the parking lot. Before retrieving my asparagus and flowers in the lobby, I called Pi to make sure he hadn't flown the coop.

"Yeah?" He sounded edgy.

"How're you doing?"

"Not good."

"What's the trouble."

"I need a beer run."

"I'll bring you some."

"When?"

I glanced at my watch. "In about an hour." I wanted to see Maggie first.

"I may not last that long."

"You shouldn't drink before noon."

"Up yours!"

"Come on, Pi. I'm working my butt off for you, and that's all you have to say?"

"No. Be sure it's cold."

I bought two six-packs at Harry's, stashed them in my saddlebags, and lumbered clumsily toward Delaware, cursing Pi all the way. Was he really worth all this? Unfortunately riding alone stimulates introspection; especially if you're forced to ride slowly. And the last thing I wanted was to open those mental compartments, those Pandora's boxes, and let out all my troubles—Tom, Maggie, Bobby, Pi. I focused on the road ahead and tried to keep my mind a blank. Into that blankness sailed a small figure on a bicycle. A familiar figure. I ground to a halt. Dragging her feet, Becca skidded to a stop.

"What are you doing here?" I demanded. We were only a stone's throw from the fisherman's shack—Pi's hideaway.

"I went to see Bobby."

"He lives around here?" I was surprised.

She nodded. "Right over there." She pointed to a nest of trees. I couldn't see any dwelling. "We saw your friend."

I gasped.

"Yeah. He was great."

"What do you mean?"

"We were horsin' around in this clearing and he was taking a sunbath. He asked Bobby where he got his shiner. Bobby didn't say anything, but I told him his dad did it. And you know what he said?"

"No." I held my breath.

"He said, 'I'd like to meet this gentleman.'" Becca did a good imitation of Pi doing his gentleman act.

"And?"

"And—" Becca's eyes sparkled, "we introduced him, and Pi told him if he ever laid a hand on Bobby again he'd come back and beat the shit out of him."

I let my breath out. "So Bobby doesn't live in Jersey? He lives in Delaware?"

"Yeah. Bobby says it works out real well because his dad doesn't have to pay Jersey taxes and the Delaware revenuers can't find him."

"You won't tell anyone you saw Pi?" I asked anxiously.

"No way. Pi made us swear to secrecy. We wrote our names in blood."

"What?"

"Yeah. He nicked our fingers with his penknife and made us sign our initials on this scrap of paper. And he said if we broke our word he'd send the Jersey Devil after us. Then he made this ugly face like he was the Jersey Devil and told us to scram."

I had trouble controlling my laughter. Meanwhile the beer on the back of my bike was growing warm. "Well, what are you waiting for? Scram!" I started my motor.

With a grin, she peddled off.

"Special Delivery!" I sang through the screen door. Pi emerged from the shack, scratching his crotch. I wondered when he'd last had a bath. His face was a deep crimson. Too much sunbathing, I guessed. "Sorry, I didn't bring any suntan lotion."

"Just give me the liquid."

I carried the two dripping six-packs up the steps and dumped them on the porch. Only after he had ripped open the first carton, popped a can, and satisfied his thirst did he speak. "Met some friends of yours."

"So I hear."

"What a turd." His term for Mr. Shoemaker. "You should see that place. Filth. Garbage. Flies. Dirty, naked kids and half-starved dogs running around."

As if *he* were the king of sanitation.

"And you know what they were eatin'?"

I shook my head.

"Muskrat!"

"Sure. That's a delicacy in these parts. They hold a muskrat dinner every fall at the firehouse."

"This was breakfast!" He made a retching noise.

When he had finally run out of indignation, I asked him about Sunny's love life. "Were any of his disgruntled ex-girlfriends at that party?"

"So . . ." He grinned. "You think poison is a woman's weapon?"

"No way," I said bristling.

He seemed to ponder my question. "There was one old lady— Wendy. Well-hung Wendy we used to call her."

"How original." I was still smarting from the poison crack.

"We looked her up in Wildwood, and brought her and a bunch of her pals back to the party. She hung around for a while, but she left early. Probably when she saw that Sunny had eyes only for you."

I grimaced.

"Why don't you go talk to her?" he said. "She sure had a motive. But I'd have thought she'd poison you, not Sunny." He grinned.

Just what I needed—a round-trip to Wildwood—at least an hour and a half away from Bayfield. "I'll think about it."

"Hey, I thought this was a matter of life 'n death?"

I couldn't tell if he was kidding or not. I told him about the beer bottle.

He was unimpressed.

"They promised they'd have the results today."

"What time?"

"Five o'clock."

He took a deep swig from his can. "I guess these . . ." he said, gesturing at the six-packs, "will last me till five."

"Till eight," I reminded him.

"Yeah, yeah. Eight. I don't wanna leave before dark."

"I'll keep you informed." I trundled off, feeling heavier than when I'd arrived, even though I'd left the six-packs behind.

By the time I got to Maggie's it was past one o'clock. Unlike last night, the road in front of the Nelson house was deserted and the curtains were drawn over the front window. I tried the door. Open. I stepped inside and called softly, "Mag?"

No answer.

I tiptoed through the empty living room, down the hall to her bedroom. The room was a mess. Bed unmade. Half-empty cups and tumblers scattered on the bureau and bedside table. Her bathrobe lay in a heap on the floor. But no Mag.

I went back to the hall and called again, louder this time.

"In here," a faint voice filtered toward me from the end of the hall.

I entered another, very different bedroom. A boy's room. Posters of rock stars on the walls. Race-car models lining both windowsills and the bureau. The bureau was painted black, and the mirror above it was covered with stickers of comic book heroes. Batman, Spider-man, et cetera. The single bookcase was stocked with CDs and videos. (DVDs had not been around when Nick left home.) The only books were a few tattered children's volumes stashed on the bottom shelf. A double bed filled most of the room, covered with a black bedspread depicting bikers on motorcycles in yellow and red. I thought how Nick would have fit in just fine with the present tenants of the Oakview Motor Lodge.

Maggie was sitting in a rocking chair next to a window that looked out on a broad field. She didn't turn but continued to stare out the window.

"I brought you something."

"Put it there." Without turning she indicated the bureau with a languid wave.

I placed my gifts on the scratched black surface and asked, "May I sit down?"

She shrugged. I sat on the edge of the bed. There was a long silence. What to say? How to begin? I didn't have to. She began.

"He used to lock himself in here with his TV and his CD player. I never knew what he was watching or what he was listening to." She rocked gently, methodically. "Maybe if I'd paid more attention. Pried a little. Made him tell me . . ."

"No, Mag. You were a fine mother. Teenagers need their space, their privacy. They hate to be spied on or told what to do."

She rocked a little faster.

After a while, I asked timidly, "Can you see him?"

"Tomorrow. Sunday is visiting day."

I moved around the bed and sat on the side closer to her.

She looked at me for the first time. "Have they found out who killed that biker?"

"Not yet. But we may have a lead." I told her about the beer bottle.

"Not much to go on."

I nodded, feeling empty and low. "There's an old girlfriend who came to the party who might have had a motive . . ."

But Maggie had lost interest. Her gaze was back on the field. "I used to sit in this chair and read to him. *Peter Rabbit, The Wizard of Oz* . . . And he loved the Bible stories. 'Noah's Ark,' 'David and Goliath.' His favorite was 'Jonah and the Whale.' He thought it would be cool to be inside a wha—" She broke suddenly. Her shoulders heaved and a sob erupted from deep inside her body, like some wild animal cry. I threw my arms around her, locking her in a hug like one of Pi's viselike bear hugs. I didn't speak, I just squeezed her, fearing if I let go, she would fly apart—into a thousand pieces.

Her sobs came in great heaving gasps and seemed to go on forever, but it was probably less than a minute. Gradually they subsided in a series of gulps and sighs. Slowly she pulled away and wiped her wet face on her sleeve. "You really have a grip." She rubbed her arms where I had held them.

"Sorry." I said.

To my surprise, she smiled. "I'm sorry, too, Jo," she said, "for the way I lashed out at you last night. I shouldn't—"

"No, Mag. You were right. I should have told you what Nick said. I was all caught up in my own selfish affairs."

We sat for a while, staring at the field of new green corn. A soft breeze smelling of May flowers came in the window, stirring the curtains. For a brief moment I think we felt at peace.

CHAPTER 35

When I left Maggie, it was only two-thirty. It was all I could do to keep from calling the lab, Peck, Pi—*somebody*! I needed answers. I was paralyzed, frustrated by not being able to take action. When I got back to my room, I called Dad. As usual he was thrilled to hear from me and, as usual, I kicked myself for not calling him more often. I wanted to tell him about Archie, but I held back. He'd only worry—and at age seventy, he didn't need that. We chatted awhile. He told me he had a new customer. A bulb and seed company. Their hundred-page, semiannual catalog would keep a roof over his head a little while longer, he said with a chuckle. I was happy. Dad without work was like a hot dog without mustard. Maybe he could put off retirement for another few years. I did tell him about Nick, because he had met the Nelsons. He was deeply distressed and promised to write to them.

When I hung up, I felt better. Maybe I would go to Wildwood. I called Pi for Wendy's number. She was staying at a cheap motel with a bunch of other old ladies. Comfort by the Sea, he thought it was called.

I burned rubber and made the trip in an hour and fifteen minutes. One thing about south Jersey roads—there was nobody on them. Traffic jams were as scarce as hens' teeth. When I found the motel, I was informed by one stoned old lady that "they're all at the beach."

Great. Wildwood was well known for its miles of beaches. And I didn't even know what Wendy looked like. The girl gave me a generic description. "Blond, nose ring, bikini . . . blue—I think . . ."

"Thanks." I decided to head straight down the street to the ocean. Maybe I'd get lucky and she'd be there.

Despite the surroundings—hot dog stands, game arcades, and cheap bars—my first glimpse of the ocean made me forget Pi and Maggie and Tom and all the rest of the problems I'd been carrying around for the past few days. God, it was beautiful. It had been a long time since I'd been to the seashore. I closed my eyes, shutting out the vendors, the crowds, the rubbish, and inhaled deeply—searching for the smell of the sea. It eluded me on the boardwalk, but as I descended the steps to the beach, the smells of popcorn, cheese steaks, and suntan lotion were whisked away by a fresh sea breeze and I could hear the rhythmic beat and shush of the waves. When I was little, Dad and I had always spent our vacations at the seashore. I missed it.

When my boots touched sand, I scanned the beach for a cluster of biker beauties. I didn't have to look far. Even though the beach was crowded, they were easy to spot, because they were the only females without umbrellas—stretched out in a row, soaking up the sun. Fear of skin cancer was for wusses—part of the female biker code, no doubt. I ambled over. There were at least three blondes with nose rings.

"Which one of you is Wendy?" I asked.

They raised their heads in unison and stared at me.

I waited.

"Who wants to know?" asked the blonde at the end of the row.

"Jo Banks," I said. "I'm trying to find out about Sunny's death."

The others laid their heads back down on their towels. The blonde on the end said, "We've been through all that with the police." She fumbled for a cigarette and lit it with some difficulty in the strong breeze.

Although all I wanted to do was take off my boots and paddle in the water, I lowered my rump on the sand next to her and said, "Tell me about you and Sunny."

She took a deep drag on her cigarette and looked away toward the sea. "Sunny and I were over ages ago," she said, in a tone that belied her statement.

"Why did you come to the party, then?"

She looked at me. "I like parties."

"You didn't come because Sunny was there?"

"Hell, no," she said. "It's a big world. Plenty of fish."

"Did you talk to him?"

"Oh, sure. He was glad to see me. But he had other things on his mind."

"Such as?"

"You—for one." She smiled wickedly. "I saw him cart you off."

I swallowed.

"And he wasn't feeling too good," she added. "Something he ate."

I was listening carefully. A seagull dived at a trash can nearby, snatched up an old french fry, and flew away. "What did he eat?"

"How should I know?"

"Well, you rode back with him. I thought maybe you all stopped for pizza or something."

"Nah. We were souped up on meds. They kill the appetite."

I nodded knowingly, as if I did meds every day. "Did you see anyone fooling with Sunny's drinks?"

Her eyes widened. "He doesn't . . . didn't . . . drink anything but beer. He couldn't afford it."

"And it would be pretty hard to poison a beer—is that what you're saying?"

"Well, yeah. You'd have to pour something into that little hole—and how could you do that before he opened it?"

"You've given this some thought—"

Her eyelids narrowed. "Say, you don't think I did Sunny in, do ya?"

"Hmm?"

She jumped up, dropping her cigarette and scattering sand. *"You bitch,"* she yelled, hands on hips.

"I don't think anything." I stood up, too. "I'm just trying to find out what happened to Sunny."

Several of the other girls were showing interest. Was one of their own under attack? I didn't see any weapons lying around, and bikinis don't leave much room for concealment. But I'd heard that some biker women were pretty good with anything sharp—broken bottles . . . I eyed the trash can. Cracked seashells . . . I scanned the sand around us.

"Sunny was a prick," yelled one of the recliners.

"Yeah," growled another. "Wendy was well rid of him."

Wendy still held her confrontational stance, and one by one the others were pulling themselves off their towels like so many self-adhesive postage stamps. I noticed their muscles. Although smaller than those of their male counterparts, the women were nothing to sneeze at. How could these people lead the lives they did and still stay fit? A good topic for a medical study—for some other doctor to tackle, some other time.

"OK. Thanks for your help." I backed away.

"Don't you want to stay and talk?" This from a woman whose arms and legs looked like they were carved from cedar or oak. They were all standing now, forming a circle around me. They outnumbered me ten to one. It was definitely time to go.

I took off, pounding the sand with my boots, frightening seagulls and little children carrying buckets. I didn't care what kind of scene I made; I wasn't about to be pulverized by a bunch of muscle-bound females. I dashed up the steps to the boardwalk. Not until I was well onto the boards, blending with the crowd, did I dare look back They were still standing, looking after me—spoiling my ocean view.

My bike had never looked so good. I mounted and started the long trek back to Bayfield. I was halfway home before I asked myself why Wildwood was so crowded in May. Then it dawned on me. It was Memorial Day Weekend.

CHAPTER 36

As I arrived at my door, I heard my phone ringing on the other side, I fumbled with my key, crashed in—stubbing my toe on the futon—and grabbed the receiver.

"Peck here."

I drew a deep breath. "Any news?"

"That sediment in the bottom of the beer bottle . . ."

My heart thumped "Yes?"

"Arsenic, and . . ."

Old lace? I waited.

"The fingerprints on the bottle belonged to Sunny—mostly."

"Mostly?"

"There were two other sets. The ones all over the neck were yours, no doubt."

"I tried to be careful."

But we couldn't match the other set to anyone in our database." He sounded disappointed.

Pi's prints were in the national database, because of his prison record. "That clears Pi then, doesn't it?"

"Whoa. These prints might belong to anyone—some guy who worked for the beer distributor, or in the deli where the beer was sold. The poisoner who handed Sunny the beer—possibly Pi—probably wore gloves, leaving no prints."

Or possibly—Jingles, Wendy, or . . . Stan

Why Stan? A scene in the parking lot had played itself out before me. Fran and Sunny—tight as two peas—on his bike. Stan popping up out of nowhere.

"What about Stan?" I said, and gave him my reason.

"What was Stan's room number?" Peck asked.

"Twenty-three." As a bonus I gave him Stan's license number.

"Good work."

UR4ME wasn't hard to remember.

"I'll get back to you." He hung up.

I glanced at my clock. Five-thirty. Still sandy and salty from my trip to the seashore, I was dying for a shower, but I called Pi first, anxious to give him the news. It rang five times before voicemail kicked in. Ohmygod. Don't tell me he'd taken off already. I ran to the parking lot and mounted my bike. Jingles sidled up to me, wearing one of his humorless smirks.

"Going somewhere?" he asked.

"What's it to you?"

". . . to see Pi?" The smirk turned into a sneer.

I'm sure I looked guilty. "What were *you* doing at that party?" I asked, turning the tables. Here was a biker ripe for some questioning. I'd been looking for one all day.

He seemed surprised. "What d'ya mean? I was the preacher. You saw me."

"Not that party. The other one."

"Boozin', dancin'—same as you. But you wouldn't dance with me—remember?" his tone was accusatory.

"Did you give Sunny something to drink?"

As it dawned on him where I was headed, his manner changed from bantering to threatening. He leaned in so close I could smell his breath—a combination of stale alcohol and bad teeth. "*Watch . . . it . . . girl.*" The three words glowed between us like hot coals.

I fired up and cruised out of the lot. Turning right, I headed in the opposite direction from Pi's hideout. A few minutes later. I heard a bike behind me and glimpsed Jingles in my left side mirror. He was gaining on me. When he came alongside, he came too close. Way too close! I leaned into the shoulder, almost tipping over. "Bastard!" I screamed.

"Hoo, hoo, hoo, hoo, hoo!" he let out one of his high-pitched squeals and tore off, narrowly missing a hay truck in front of me. *Asshead.*

As soon as Jingles was out of sight, I made a U-turn and headed for Pi. Of course he might have had his cell phone turned off. But being out of touch made me nervous. Peck had warned that Pi wasn't out of the woods yet (an apt expression), and there was always the possibility of extradition.

As I rode, I tried to sort things out. Opportunity, means, and motive—I recited the familiar litany for a murder investigation. Then I applied it to the three suspects: Jingles, Wendy, and Stan.

They all had opportunity. They were all at the party. They all had means. The rat poison was in the motel closet. But Jingles and Stan were more apt to know of its whereabouts than Wendy, who had just arrived. And by the time the party started, the closets were probably closed and locked. Maybe she had brought her own supply, I thought maliciously.

As for motive, Jingles had the strongest. Power. He wanted Pi's job. King of the club. What better way to get rid of Pi than to stick him with a murder rap. And Jingles was probably the only one who knew about Pi's prison record. Wendy's motive was easy—sexual jealousy. If she couldn't have Sunny, then no one else should. And Stan? Again, the image of Sunny and Fran—squeezed together on his bike seat—flashed before me.

Then there was the matter of character. Not everyone is capable of murder. Or are they? Given the right circumstances? Jingles certainly was. He wore the 1-percent patch. He had killed at least one person. Maybe more. They say it gets easier each time. And of all the bikers, he was the only one I could imagine using poison. He was sneaky.

Wendy? She was tough. She might even have a mean streak. But a killer? It was hard to judge on such a short acquaintance, but my gut feeling was no. Some of her pals would have been better candidates. But they had no motive. Of course Pi would say the choice of weapon—poison—pointed to a woman. The hell with him.

That left Stan. His character wasn't hard to read. A wimpy whiner, weighted down by years with a fickle wife. Not exactly a man of action. Someone who would commit murder.

A phrase from Jack's manuscript suddenly came to me. How had he put it?

The little green man comes in many guises. He can come like a worm in an apple—or like a fire in the furnace.

In Stan's case, he could have come both ways. Nibbling like a worm over the years as Fran indulged in her silly dalliances, then suddenly Sunny was one too many—the proverbial last straw—and the fire in the furnace kicked in.

Deep in my thoughts as I sped through the corridor of phragmites that led to the shack, I didn't notice the red lights spinning or hear the shouts until I broke into the clearing. Two patrol cars were parked by the door and four troopers were clustered around the porch like flies.

"Come out with your hands up," Trooper #1 shouted.

I pulled to a stop and shut off my motor. "What's going on?" I shouted.

Trooper #1 turned, followed by the others.

"What d'ya know? The girlfriend shows up. Good timing. *Another reason for you to come out!*" he yelled into the shack.

"Stay where you are, Pi!" I yelled, spreading my glare among the troopers. "I told you, you can't touch him," I addressed Trooper #1.

"That out-of-state line doesn't hold up anymore!" he said, flapping a sheaf of papers at me. "We got the documents to extradite him."

"Let me see those." I dismounted and walked over to him. The other troopers were grinning. To my dismay, the papers looked authentic. A warrant signed by the governor and several other high state officials. When I looked up, Pi was on the porch staring at me.

"I don't know about this . . ." I said hesitantly.

"Sure, you don't know. You don't know shit from Shinola." He took the cuffs off his belt and shook the screen door. "Come on, Apple Pie, or whatever your name is. You're comin' with us."

I saw Pi tense. I knew he was contemplating making a run for it, out the back door, where his bike was parked. But common sense prevailed. He knew they were armed, and he wasn't suicidal. Slowly he unhooked the screen door and stood aside to let them in.

They cuffed him and hauled him down the steps. As they shoved him into a patrol car, he muttered to me, "Take care of my bike," and pressed his keys into my hand. (He must have taken them from his pocket before they cuffed him.) He seemed unruffled, except for one thing—no one but me, or maybe his mother, would have noticed it. When Archie was a boy, he had a habit of swallowing repeatedly when he was upset. In those days his neck was skinny and you could see his Adam's apple shooting up and down spasmodically. When Pi had pressed his bike keys into my hand, I'd seen a repeated ripple under the now taut skin of his full neck

"We'll have you out in no time!" I growled.

He nodded. I think he actually trusted me. *Damn. Damn. Damn.* And I had no idea how I could back up my words.

After they left, I rode around to the rear of the shack, parked my bike, and mounted Pi's. In the midst of misery there were always a few bonuses. I roared off.

CHAPTER 37

A patrol car was in front of the motel. (I couldn't get away from them.) Paul was at the desk, looking drained and frail. Marie was sitting stiffly on the sofa looking furious. No bikers. They were probably at the local bars getting an early start on Saturday night.

"What's up?" I asked.

"The police are searching room twenty-three, the one next to yours, for fingerprints," Paul said wearily.

"I'm done with my shift, but they won't let me go home," Marie burst out. "They say I cleaned that room too good." She was indignant.

I had to laugh. "That's a backhanded compliment, Marie. You should be happy,"

She glowered.

"Is Peck here?"

"He's here," Paul said.

"He's the one who told me I take my cleaning too seriously!" Marie piped up.

"I'll see what I can do." I had a bone of my own to pick with Peck.

. . .

He was leaning against the doorjamb of room 23, supervising. Over his shoulder, I glimpsed two forensics, a man and a woman, working like beavers with an array of complicated equipment.

I confronted Peck. "What's the big idea?"

He turned and drawled, "Just doing my job."

"I don't mean this. I mean arresting Pi."

"Just doing my job," he repeated.

"I thought you'd hold off at least till you checked out this guy." I tapped the number 23 tacked to the door.

"Can't leave any stone unturned," he said sanctimoniously.

I wanted to slug him. But I also wanted to find out the results of the search. I decided not to push it. "How's this going?" I asked.

He frowned. "Nothing so far. The maids are too conscientious in this dump."

"Careful. You're speaking of my home."

"Sorry." He didn't look sorry.

"What about Stan?"

"We sent some people to Cherry Hill to pick him up."

I felt better. "Arrest him?"

"We don't have enough evidence for an arrest. They're just bringing him in for questioning."

"Will you be able to get his prints?"

"Not without his consent."

Damn. "What happens next?"

"We'll be done here in a few minutes," he said disconsolately. "Then we go back to headquarters and wait."

I wasn't the only one who had to wait, I realized. Suddenly I had an idea. "Excuse me." I darted into my room, grabbed my box of surgical gloves, and headed for the basement.

The motel basement was an enormous cinderblock space used for storage: carpet remnants, insulating material, tools, etc. Paul had a workbench down here, where he and I had once concocted a scarecrow. It seemed like a lifetime ago. The end nearest the stairs was filled with dark green trash bags. At least thirty of them. Trash was picked up Tuesdays and Fridays. There was no way to identify which rooms or even which floors the bags had come from. They weren't neatly labeled by room number—21, 22, 23. I groaned and attacked the nearest bag.

Sixteen bags and three pairs of surgical gloves later, I located the bourbon bottles. I lifted one carefully and set it on the bottom step. I refilled the last trash bag, retied it with a twistum, and clasping the bottle gingerly by the neck, returned to room 23.

They were just finishing up. The forensics were packing their equipment and Peck was watching them with a dejected expression.

"Try this."

"Huh?"

I pushed the brown bottle at him. "I took it from one of Stan's trash baskets. I'll bet it's loaded with prints."

He called the male forensic over and told him to test the bottle. He was annoyed at having to unpack again. Sure enough—a perfect set of prints emerged! The specialist handed the bottle to his female partner who wrapped it carefully in a paper sack and labeled it "evidence." With a look that bordered on respectful, Peck said, "I'll be in touch."

CHAPTER 38

And he was. He called me an hour later and asked me to come to Headquarters to sit in on Stan's inquiry. He didn't have to ask twice.

Peck met me at the door and briefed me quickly on my role. This was to be an informal interview, not a formal interrogation. (I would not have been allowed to attend the latter.) He wanted me to sit as quietly and unobtrusively as possible, listen, and observe. Afterward he would ask my opinion of what took place.

Eager to take part, no matter how passive my role, I agreed to everything. He ushered me into a small, bland room with three chairs and a desk. He took the chair behind the desk and gestured for me to take the chair to one side. The chair facing the desk remained empty for Stan.

I was barely seated before I heard two pairs of footsteps in the corridor. One solid and firm, the other lighter and less sure. A police officer ushered Stan into the room. The officer stepped back, taking a place by the door, and Stan stood blinking uncertainly. When he recognized me, he looked puzzled, but he said nothing.

"Please sit down, Mr. Huntsburger," Peck said.

So Stan had a last name.

"I apologize for the inconvenience of bringing you down here. I just have a few questions . . ."

Stan forced a smile.

"I've asked Dr. Banks to join us primarily because she is familiar with the motel's physical plant, the staff, and so forth, and I thought if you had any questions, she could answer them better than I."

Stan and I stared uncomfortably at each other.

He was more dressy today than at the motel. Instead of shorts, T-shirt, and sneakers, he wore a light suit, sport shirt, and loafers. He must have come straight from work. I wondered what his work was. At the motel I had taken his flushed face for sunburn, but in the bright overhead lights, it looked more like the flush of the chronic alcoholic.

"Leave the door open, will you Mike?" Peck said to the officer who had been about to close the door. The detective folded his hands on the desk and leaned forward. "Let's get this over with as quickly as possible," he said. "Could you tell me where you were the night Robert "Sunny" Parker died?"

So Sunny had a last name, too.

"I was at the motel," he said. "My wife and I were staying there. I think I told you that, Mr. Peck." He was faintly accusatory.

"You probably did. But my mind is a sieve." Peck spoke affably.

Stan relaxed slightly.

If Peck was the good cop, then, was I the bad cop?

"What I meant was," Peck continued, "where specifically were you—say from six o'clock to midnight? In your room, the lobby, the parking lot?"

"All three. Fran and I grabbed a bite at the Clam Shell, a little place outside of Salem. Has great seafood. Then we came back to the motel to watch TV. There was some program Fran wanted to see. But the racket outside our window was so loud, we couldn't hear it. We shut it off and Fran picked up a mystery, but I went down to the lobby to see what was going on."

"What *was* going on?" Peck asked.

"You know. Those bikers were all jazzed up—drinking and yelling. I wouldn't be surprised if they were doing drugs. It was a riot!" He looked nervous just talking about it.

"So what did you do then, Mr. Huntsburger?"

"Nothing. I just stood around in the lobby and the parking lot watching them, trying to stay out of their way. Jack-the-Night-Clerk was on desk duty. A lot a good he did. Acted like a scared rabbit."

"And what about you? Were you scared?"

"Of course not," Stan huffed. "I was just annoyed that my wife couldn't watch her TV show. You pay good money for a room, the least you expect is a little peace and quiet."

"Why *were* you staying in Bayfield, of all places," Peck asked with a smile.

I marveled at Peck's easy-going manner. But he had said this was to be an informal interview.

"I was working on a deal for my storage company, looking for some cheap real estate to build new units. It was supposed to bring in big bucks. It's hard to keep a lady like mine in mink, you know." He grinned. "Why else would anyone go to such a godforsaken place? The night life?" He risked a little joke.

"Why would you bring your wife to such a 'godforsaken place'?" Peck pursued.

"She needed a little vacation—a change of scene. She doesn't do well cooped up in the house. Besides, I like to keep a close eye on her." He winked at Peck. "She's a wild one."

"Did you see the victim, Sunny, when you were hanging out in the lobby?" Peck adopted a more businesslike tone.

"Oh, sure. He was in and out. They'd stashed some of the booze there and they all came in for refills."

"What kind of booze?"

"Beer, mostly. But there was hard stuff too. Vodka and bourbon. Some of them hit the soda machine for mixers."

"About how long were you there?"

He shrugged.

"Approximately?"

"About an hour. Long enough to see Sunny carry the doctor off." He snickered, glanced at me, then blushed.

"Did you see Mr. Canby nick Sunny's ear with an arrow?" Peck asked.

"Yeah. But I didn't know what happened at the time. The arrow didn't make any noise and all I saw was a lot of commotion. Then one of the bikers rushed in and called nine-one-one. He asked for an ambulance. I thought things were getting too hot, so I went back to my room."

A dispatcher stuck his head in the doorway and asked to speak to Peck. The detective excused himself. An awkward silence stretched between Stan and me, but I'd be damned if I'd break it. Finally Stan said, "What are you doin' in Bayfield, Doctor?"

"I live and practice here." I said.

"I mean, what's a highly educated woman like you doin' at a two star motel in the boondocks?" He sent me a knowing look. "Hidin' out?"

"I beg your pardon?"

"Oh, sorry. I didn't mean anything." He backed off quickly. "I just thought you might have some malpractice problems or something . . ." he trailed off.

I glared at him.

"Ok, ok." He raised his hands in mock self-defense.

We sat in strained silence until Peck returned.

This time the detective went straight to the point. Looking directly at Stan, he said, "When you were in the lobby, did you ever, at any time, give Sunny something to drink?"

"What d'ya mean?" Stan sat up.

"I mean, when Sunny came into the lobby for a refill, did you ever hand him a beer?"

"No way. The bottles were sitting right there in the cooler."

"Did you tamper with one of those beers? Twist open the bottle and introduce some toxic substance—"

"Now why would I do that?" His look of amazement seemed genuine, but bands of sweat were visible under both arms. "I didn't even know the guy."

"Your wife did," I interjected.

Both Stan and Peck looked at me, and Stan's face drained of color.

"Let's take a break," Peck said abruptly. "How about a Coke, Mr. Huntsburger?"

Momentarily deaf, Stan stared at his shoe tips.

"A Coke?" Peck repeated.

He glanced up. "Uh . . . oh, sure."

Peck rose and gestured for me to follow him into the hall. The police officer remained behind with Stan.

When we were outside, I said, "I'm really sorry. It just came out."

"No harm done. What did you mean by that comment?"

"Remember, I told you. His wife took a long ride with Sunny on his bike and Stan was there when they got back. Did you notice how pale he was after I spoke?"

Peck nodded, and was thoughtful. "I think I'd better take it alone from here. You can go home—"

"Do I have to?" I was disappointed. The interview was just beginning to get interesting.

"'Fraid so." He looked at me. "We have to go carefully now, stay within legal limits. He may be on the verge of a confession and I don't want any foul-ups. Go home and get some rest. I'll keep you posted."

"But he was just about to break—"

"When I suggested a Coke, I did that because it's time for this interview to become official. I didn't expect things to move so fast. Your comment accelerated things. You were a big help." He winked and headed for the Coke machine.

I lingered in the hall. I didn't like being dismissed so unceremoniously. But it was my own fault. I should have kept my mouth shut. But I wondered about Peck. I didn't trust him completely. He had broken his promise about bringing the law to the funeral. Maybe he didn't want a confession? Did he still think Pi killed Sunny? I walked to my bike—Pi's bike—head down, intent on my thoughts.

"Hi, Doc."

"Mickey. What are you doing here?"

"A bunch of us came down to see if we could fix bail for Pi."

"And?"

"No soap. No bail for somebody held on a murder charge."

I knew that.

"What are you doin' here?"

"Uh . . ." Better not say too much. "Peck asked me to drop by and answer a few questions."

"You ain't a suspect, are you?"

I laughed. "Hope not."

"I thought I saw them bringing in that Mr. Milktoast from the motel. The one with the hot old lady."

"Oh?" I played innocent.

"She sure was some chick. I'll bet that wuss has trouble keepin' her out of the sack—with other dudes, that is." He snorted.

"Umm. Did you see Pi?"

"Naw. No visitors for twenty-four hours after an arrest. This place is a fuckin' concentration camp!" He slapped his leather glove against his palm. "Well, as they say, I'll see you back at the ranch." Mickey ambled off to get his bike.

As I tried to fall asleep, a wave of nausea swept over me. I thought of Pi, alone, pacing a small brick cell, expecting me to rescue him. *"Get some rest,"* Peck had said. *Sure, Detective.* At least I didn't have to worry about Pi skipping town tonight. He was safely incarcerated. And *he* didn't have to worry about mosquitoes! As I said, even when life is the worst, there are sometimes compensations.

Stan's words bored in on me. *"What are you doin' in Bayfield, Doctor? Hidin' out?"* *Compartmentalize!* That compartment is closed and locked, if you plan to get any sleep tonight.

I sat up and turned on the light. In desperation, I picked up Jack's story and began to read. This time I finished it. Jack was a good writer, and I couldn't wait to tell him. I threw on my old wrapper and went down to the lobby. He was asleep, his head on the desk. I shook him gently. "Hey Jack!"

He looked at me, groggy. "What's up?"

I waved his manuscript at him. "This is good! Gotta send it out. Don't leave it in a drawer—or some filing cabinet."

"You mean it?" He was wide awake.

"Absolutely."

A serene smile spread across his face.

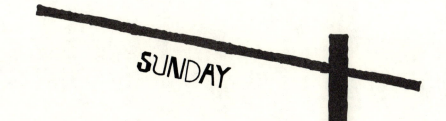
SUNDAY

CHAPTER 39

The shrill sound of the alarm interrupted my dream. It had been a good dream, too. Tom and I were back together, having a few beers at Harry's. The shrill sound came again. Not the alarm. The phone.

"Yes?"

"We broke him." Peck.

"When?"

"A few minutes ago." I looked at the clock. Two-twenty A.M. "That tip you gave us about his wife taking a ride with Sunny? We needled him about it and he finally collapsed like a bowlful of Jell-O. It was kind of pathetic, actually. Apparently this dame had been teasing him for years. Playing around with other guys, but not really—you know what I mean?"

"Yes."

"Something snapped inside Stan this week, and Sunny paid for a long line of suitors," he said.

"Is Pi free?"

"Officially. But he has to wait till morning for us to complete the paperwork."

"Can I see him?"

" 'Fraid not. House rules."

"Can't you bend them? If I hadn't mentioned that joy ride his wife took—

"Sorry." He cleared his throat and said in a slightly embarrassed tone, "One thing we couldn't get out of him is how he got Sunny's beer bottle back. Any ideas about that?"

"No problem. Those guys never throw anything in the trash—they just drop it wherever they happen to be when they're finished with it. Stan probably hung around till Sunny dropped the bottle, then picked it up. If anyone saw him, they wouldn't have thought anything of it."

"Huh. And then, Einstein that he is, he stashed it in the cupboard, planning to pick it up later."

"Yeah." I laughed. "But he forgot."

"Thanks."

After he hung up, more of Jack's words came back to me again.

"The little green man...can nibble at your insides over a period of months and years or burst on you, searing you in an instant.

Poor Stan.

The brick jail, vintage 1890, was tucked behind the courthouse. The plumbing hadn't been updated since, I'd heard. I parked my bike and went inside.

"I'm here to pick up . . . Pi. They brought him in last night."

The man at the desk looked blank.

"Big fellow. Heavyset. Long hair. Nose ring. Earring. Tattoos."

Light dawned. "Oh, that guy. He left."

"What?"

He glanced at his watch. "Yeah, he's been gone over an hour."

"But he didn't have his bike. How could he leave?"

"I think the detective gave him a lift."

I barreled back to the motel, breaking the speed limit in my usual coy fashion. When I burst into the lobby, I stopped short. Maggie was at the front desk.

"Hi, Mag."

She looked gray and wan. But it was good she'd made the effort. She smiled—barely.

"Have you seen any bikers this morning?"

Frowning, she shook her head, a sign that she still disapproved of my associating with them.

I went back to the parking lot. I couldn't understand it. Where could he be? Knowing Pi, the first thing he would want after he was sprung was his bike. I jogged around the parking lot a few times. Still no Pi. I went back in the lobby and had a cup of coffee swill. Maggie was deep in a romance novel. I flipped through the *Bugle*. Nick's story was on page 3. He was awaiting his appeal. If Pi didn't come soon, I'd have to go to the hospital on *his* bike. I was fuming. I had patients to see. Life didn't stop because of one biker's little problems.

Pi burst through the lobby door.

"Where have you been?" I demanded.

"In jail." He grinned.

"I mean, since then. I came to get you."

"With my bike?"

I nodded.

"Good girl." He came and gave me a bear hug. "I hear I owe you. Peck says you helped nail that asshole."

"You didn't answer my question."

"I went to see your boyfriend."

"Tom?"

"He's the man of the moment, ain't he?"

"How'd you get there?"

"Peck dropped me off and I hitched a ride back here."

"But why—"

"I had to straighten things out. I told him what that kiss amounted to—!"

I was speechless.

"I told him I always give the chicks a friendly buss, to test them out. If they respond . . . it's full speed ahead. If not . . . no harm done. But when I bussed you, it was like kissing the underbelly of a dead codfish . . ."

"Pi!"

"And believe me, I've bussed my share of chicks."

"Pi, spare me!"

"What's the matter? I fixed everything with you and your boyfriend. You should be foot-kissin' grateful."

I sighed.

"Hey, you hang on to that guy. He's righteous. I can smell it. Pretty soon, thanks to me, he'll trundle over here, hat in hand, ready to eat crow."

"Oh, my god." I slumped on the sofa.

"One good turn deserves another." He punched my shoulder as if I were one of his buddies. (I'd be black-and-blue for days.) "Now where's my bike?"

"In the lot." I tossed him his keys.

When he left, I glanced over at Maggie. She had laid her romance novel aside. "*Your* love life is more interesting," she said, with a ghost of her former twinkle.

As I heard Pi revving his bike, I remembered *my* bike! I rushed out to the lot, waving frantically. "Wait! My bike's at the shack. You've gotta take me."

"Hop on."

I hopped on the back, gripping him around the waist. The sound of a Harley allows for no conversation. We rode in silence. But once at the shack, I asked when he was leaving.

"We'll be heading out tonight after," he paused, ". . . some unfinished business."

"What . . . ?" I felt cold.

He looked at me, deciding how much to tell. Finally he said, "Jingles. He ID'd me at the funeral. Remember when he gave me that big kiss?"

I remembered.

"That was the signal for the troopers to take me."

I let that sink in. "You mean he snitched?"

He nodded.

"But why . . . ?"

"Power. You were right. He wanted my job."

"How did you find out?"

"One of the troopers let it out. He was gloating about it on the way to that quaint little jail of yours—the one that serves a free roach with every meal."

"What are you going to do?" I had blocked on Pi's new capacity for violence. Something acquired since his paper boy days.

He didn't answer.

"Be careful. You'll end up back in that quaint little jail."

He laughed at that. "The law don't care if a biker beats up another biker. In fact, it makes them happy, 'cause they'd like to do it themselves."

I tried again. "Might doesn't make right."

His expression hardened. "Save that crap for Sunday school." He mounted his bike.

"Pi—"

"So long. And don't forget, I owe you. You have my cell number." With a high sign, he kick-started his bike and twisted the throttle.

Ears throbbing, I watched the Harley disappear between the banks of phragmites.

Tom didn't come with hat in hand. (I don't think he owned one.) But he did call. With no preamble, he asked me to a dance. "Wear a skirt," he told me. "And not one of those itty-bitty things that cling like Saran Wrap. A long, full skirt that flows and swirls with the music."

"And where am I going to find a skirt like that?"

"That's up to you."

I was so happy to hear from him, I decided to try to please him. I looked around my motel room for something I could convert into a long skirt. I knew my closet had nothing to offer. I wandered into the bathroom. The shower curtain was kind of cute. Little yellow ducks swimming in a blue sea. It had come with the territory. I had been meaning to replace it but never got around to it. After giving it a shake, I decided it was too heavy and would probably be as hot as hell.

In my Manhattan days, an invitation to a dance would have meant a quick trip to Sak's or Bloomies—and returning at least three hundred bucks poorer.

Back in the main room, I passed my linen closet—a fancy name for the cubbyhole in the wall that held my ragged sheets and towels. I flipped through the towels—faded yellow, blue, and salmon with stringy edges, sporting an occasional hole the size of a half dollar. I pulled out a threadbare beach towel. You could still make out a shadow of Snoopy dancing on it. With it wrapped around my waist, the effect was more that of a sarong than a ball gown. Dorothy Lamour I am not.

Under the towels lay one of my two sets of sheets. (The other set was on my futon.) White, with a pattern of turquoise butterflies, it might do. I had a turquoise top that I wore only on special occasions. Weddings, funerals (not biker funerals). I began pulling together my ensemble. I figured if I poked holes along the edge of the sheet with my surgical scissors and pulled a drawstring through it, it could return to its sheet role after the ball without suffering too much damage. Sandals would have to take the place of glass slippers. I made a vow to be home by midnight, before I turned into a pumpkin—or worse: a squash or turnip. I grabbed the sheet, the scissors, and set to work.

Half an hour later everything was ready except the drawstring. I rummaged through my catch-all drawer, the one reserved for thumbtacks, old wine corks, Scotch tape—ah yes, and a ball of twine. Becca and I had bought it one windy day when we had decided to fly a kite. The kite had ended up tangled in some telephone wires, à la Charlie Brown, but we'd gotten a lot of exercise. Bayfield was probably one of the last places on earth that had telephone wires above ground. It was also one of the last places where kids still flew kites, rode bikes, and played baseball on their own, without being organized, supervised, and criticized by an overzealous parent group. *What's with you? You don't even have kids.*

When I was dressed and stood before the full-length mirror on the back of my bathroom door, I had to admit I looked quite fetching. A pair of hoop earrings would complete the picture. With a farewell pirouette to my reflection (which almost sent me sprawling), I went to hunt up those earrings.

CHAPTER 40

When Tom had called, he told me instead of meeting me at Harry's as usual, he would pick me up—in his *pickup*. "This is going to be a real date," he said.

I felt silly standing around the lobby all gussied up, especially with some bikers still milling around. Hash Brown asked, "Gotta big date?" And Honey bid me, "Have a hot time!" I sat curled up on the sofa, trying to hide behind a copy of the *Bugle,* which I'd already read from cover to cover. I kept an ear cocked for Tom's horn, but he came into the lobby in person, wearing real trousers, a white shirt, and a pair of brown oxfords. I almost fainted. His expression told me he was just as shocked by my appearance. It was the first time we had seen each other in anything but jeans and tees.

He held out his arm. I took it, feeling as awkward as a teenager going to her first prom. I kept my head down as we crossed the parking lot, hoping a stray biker wouldn't spot me. Once in the pickup, I breathed a sigh of relief.

"What's the matter?" He looked at me, his key halfway to the ignition.

"Nothing." I felt a blush begin,

"Not used to dressing up, huh? Well, neither am I." He poked a finger inside his collar, to give himself more breathing room.

I laughed. "This was your idea," I reminded him.

"Damned right. You can't go to the Starlight Room dressed like a farmhand."

It was my turn to look at him.

"Remember me telling you I was making a surprise for you?"

I stretched my mind back a few aeons, to that night when we had shopped together at the supermarket. "Oh, yeah."

"Well, it's finished—and tonight's the night."

"Hmm," I smiled, getting the message—our recent differences were off-limits, at least for tonight.

I was surprised when Tom drove into his own driveway. I was familiar with his simple farmhouse. Nothing new about that. Could the surprise be that there was *no* surprise? I kept quiet and let him help me down from the truck, feeling as if I were in a play, acting the part of an ingenue, on her first date.

Once inside, I saw the wooden kitchen table that he had made, set with a cloth, wineglasses, and candles. The scent of something delicious wafted from the oven. What was it? I sniffed.

"Roast chicken and corn bread," he answered my unasked question.

"Umm."

"Sit down." He pulled out my chair and poured a sparkling wine.

Holy Moly, I could get used to this.

Over dinner, we caught up on each other's past. Even though we had been apart only four days, there was a lot of ground to cover. I told him about the biker funeral, being chased by troopers, my visit to Wildwood, Pi's incarceration, and Stan's confession. Tom told me about Nick's sentencing (he had gone to the courthouse), the postmortem party at the Nelsons', and his visit with Nick. He had gone to see him after the sentencing, for old times' sake.

"What did you think of that 'born again' bunk?" I asked.

He looked at me so long, I began to feel uncomfortable. Then he said, "Did it ever occur to you, Dr. Banks, that there's a whole universe out there that you may know nothing about?" He rose.

"Which brings me to my surprise." He took my hand and led me up the crooked wooden stairs to his loft. I had been there before, a large, spare room with windows on all four sides, overlooking fields in every direction. Tonight the fields were dark, but during the day, in spring and summer, the room was like a ship's cabin and the green fields like ocean waves, shimmering in the sun. As I emerged from the dark stairwell into the loft, something felt different. There was a greater feeling of space than even before. I looked up and drew a quick breath. Where once there had been a solid roof, now there was open sky. The stars crowded one another—pushing, pulsing, shooting, showering, going about their busy, brilliant lives in the dark sky. I saw the Big and Little Dippers, Orion, and the Ram, outlined as clearly as on a page in an astronomy book. And there was no moon tonight to drown them out. (Had he planned it that way?) Bending my head back, I spun around, trying to take in the whole sky at once. From somewhere music began to play. Melodies from long ago. Dance music that my father used to listen to on our old record player. Benny Goodman, Glen Miller, Tommy Dorsey. Tom took me in his arms and we danced.

But this music wasn't from records. Over Tom's shoulder, I tracked its source to a small radio tucked into a bookshelf. The program was on every Sunday night, he told me. It was called *The Starlight Room.* From 8:00 PM till midnight, they played tunes from the thirties and forties, the heyday of the famous dance bands. The MC was a charming old codger who knew the history of these bands, the bandleaders, and the composers of the tunes. Every now and then, he would interrupt the music and give us some of his knowledge in a quiet, unassuming voice. We used these interludes to pause and catch our breath.

During one of these intermissions, Tom demonstrated the skylight roof. He had removed the old wooden roof and replaced it with thermal glass that you could slide open or shut, depending on the weather. "Like the sunroof in a car," he explained. He had even included a screen to keep the mosquitoes out. Tonight, because it was mild, he had opened the roof all the way and it seemed, if you stood on tiptoe, you could literally touch the stars.

During another break, he pushed me away and examined me through narrowed lids. "I've been meaning to tell you what a lovely skirt you're wearing. How did you come up with it on such short notice?"

I told him.

He laughed and drew me close.

Sometime during the evening, when I was mellow with music and wine, I asked, "Why did you follow me that night?"

"I was worried about you. I was afraid you were in over your head."

"Protecting me?" An accusatory note crept into my voice.

"Ah," he said, and smiled, "press the right button and out pops the outraged feminist. Yes, Jo, I wanted to look after you, the way I would look after anyone I care about—man, woman, or child. Not because I thought you were the 'weaker sex.' As you have often told me, sex and friendship are two different things. Wouldn't you do the same for me?"

After a pause, I said, "You were really wrought up that night in the parking lot. I was . . . a little afraid of you."

He closed his eyes, as if trying to recall that distant moment When he spoke his tone was playful. "You needn't of feared me. My Momma always told me, 'Women are special. You can love 'em and leave 'em. But never strike them.' "

"She was ahead of her time."

After a pause, I asked, "Would you have called me, if Pi hadn't explained things?" I didn't really want to know.

He looked me straight in the eye. "No," he said.

"Why did you believe him?"

"Whatever Pi's faults, dishonesty isn't one of them." He placed his hand gently over my mouth. "Enough, Jo. Let's enjoy the rest of the evening."

The music had started up again and he spun me around the room.

At midnight, as the MC was signing off, I had an epiphany. That freedom the bikers were always talking about? *Tom had it—and never talked about it.* He lived by himself, in a house he had built with his own hands. He worked for himself, beholden to no one. And he did this with no support from any organization, club, or buddy system and with no visible crutches—bikes, colors, codes, or patches. He was really independent. A one-man show—a free agent. Like the frontiersmen of long ago.

Come to think of it . . . so was I.

"What are you thinking about?" Tom came up behind me and stroked the back of my neck.

I turned, ready to tell him. But the last number of the evening had begun. He pulled me to him and we did a slow dance, joined as if we were one.

"You know what I like about this place?" he murmured.

"No. What?"

"Nobody ever cuts in."

We danced and danced, long after the Starlight Room had signed off and the only music was Tom humming in my ear. When my feet gave out, I danced with my bare feet resting on top of his bare feet. When *his* feet gave out, we dragged his mattress up from the porch and fell asleep under the fading stars and the patchwork quilt his great-great grandmother had made.

As the first light of dawn filtered through the open roof, I woke feeling rested and content. Tom woke and turned my face toward his. We kissed, as if for the first time.

MONDAY

EPILOGUE

An evening like that *had* to be followed by a beautiful morning! And it was. Unfortunately, it was a Monday morning. A workday. Tom dropped me back at the motel. I showered and dressed. As I donned my one and only pantsuit, a familiar sound drew me to the window. The bikers were lined up in the parking lot, their colorful helmets gleaming in the sun, revving their motors, preparing to take off. Pi's "unfinished business" must have taken longer than he thought it would. He had told me they would be leaving last night. There were a couple of the boys that I would have liked to say good-bye to. Mickey and Honey. But not enough to tear down to the parking lot half-naked. If this were a B movie, I would have sailed down— half-clad as I was—and whispered in Pi's ear, "Go back to school, Archie." But it wasn't a movie and I stayed at the window. As I watched, one by one they bumped out of the lot, Pi's glossy red helmet leading the pack. When the last one had disappeared down the road, an eerie silence fell over the lot and the motel. I turned back to my room and continued dressing.

Because it was such a beautiful morning, I decided to take the long way to the hospital, using the back roads. They were lined with wildflowers this time of year. The blue asters were my favorite.

And this morning they glistened with dew. "Oh, what a beautiful morning! Oh, what a beautiful day!" I couldn't help singing.

A movement by the side of the road caught my eye. A muskrat or woodchuck? I turned down the throttle and scanned the ditch. Slowly a man's head appeared.

Jingles.

I barely recognized him. His clothes were torn and covered with mud. He must have been lying in the ditch all night. His face was swollen, distorted, and stained with blood. His leather vest was gone—along with his colors. All he wore was jeans and a torn tee. I came to a full stop.

"Can I help?"

He looked up. One eye was swollen shut. There was a gash down his left cheek, oozing blood. When he recognized me, he sent a stream of foul saliva my way.

I stood my ground. "You need medical attention." I took out my cell and started to punch in 911.

"Stop! Bitch!" His voice was inhuman, the high-pitched squeal of a small mammal—a cat or a rabbit—in pain.

I put my cell away.

He struggled to climb out of the ditch and fell back. Involuntarily I reached out to help him. Again he spit. I drew back.

Again and again, I watched him struggle to climb out of the shallow ditch. A child could have done it easily. A healthy child. Finally he made it. He remained crouched on all fours, panting. When he had caught his breath, he raised his head and cast me a look brimming with hate.

As I watched his bent figure slouch down the road toward Bridgeton, stumbling every few steps, I felt a clinical remorse for his battered and broken body but nothing more. I punched 911 and gave them his location. He couldn't go far. They would find him. Who had done this? Pi . . . alone? Or had each biker taken his turn? Maybe Tom was right—they were animals. I turned my bike and rode off in the opposite direction.

. . .

The dew had dried on the asters. They no longer glistened. But they were still blue. I decided to visit Miss Snow before going to the hospital. She would be a tonic after this depressing episode. Besides, I wanted to thank her for telling me about the fisherman's shack. It had served a purpose. In anticipation of seeing my elderly patient—and friend—I turned up the throttle.

2/05

④ 2/06   7/06

④ 2/06   2/07